Will the r

Randy's eyes ~~........ ....~~ ...... and a look of recognition flashed over his features. "That you, Mister Jennum?"

Travis turned slowly to look into the young man's eyes. "No," he said. "I am Clint Adams."

For a second, the kid looked as though he didn't know what to make of the words he'd just heard. First, he looked confused, and then a smile drifted onto his face. "That's a good one, Mister Jennum," he said with a chuckle. "If you don't got your key, I can wait until tomorrow to fetch your wagon, but otherwise I gotta—"

The rest of the kid's words were cut off as Travis's hand clamped around his throat. Once he had a solid grip on the young man's neck, Travis pulled him closer . . . and squeezed just a little tighter with every word he spoke.

"Don't . . . you . . . laugh . . . at . . . me."

Randy's face went pale and then started turning red. He tried to pull Travis's hand away from his throat, but couldn't pry the other man's fingers away from his windpipe.

Glaring into Randy's eyes, Travis savored the crunch he could feel of collapsing tissues beneath the younger man's flesh. As he tightened his grip, he thought of all the times he'd been treated with similar disrespect. "That ain't gonna happen no more." He hissed. "Nobody laughs at Clint Adams."

THE GUNSMITH

241

PLAYING FOR BLOOD

J. R. ROBERTS

JOVE BOOKS, NEW YORK

This is a work of fiction. Names, characters, places, and incidents either are the product of the author's imagination or are used fictitiously, and any resemblance to actual persons, living or dead, business establishments, events, or locales is entirely coincidental.

PLAYING FOR BLOOD

A Jove Book / published by arrangement with
the author

PRINTING HISTORY
Jove edition / January 2002

Visit our website at
www.penguinputnam.com

ISBN: 0-515-13233-0

A JOVE BOOK®
Jove Books are published by The Berkley Publishing Group,
a division of Penguin Putnam Inc.,
375 Hudson Street, New York, New York 10014.
JOVE and the "J" design
are trademarks belonging to Penguin Putnam Inc.

PRINTED IN THE UNITED STATES OF AMERICA

10 9 8 7 6 5 4 3 2 1

ONE

The only reason Clint Adams had been sitting at the black-jack table was because there was nobody around who wanted to play poker. After waiting for two hours for some decent competition, Clint got tired of sitting at a table by himself and he'd played so much solitaire that the cards were starting to blur in his eyes.

The night before had been fairly busy, with him coming out on top of a five-handed game that had lasted for over thirty-six hours. It was the first time in a good long while that he'd been able to play an honest game, and the time spent was like a vacation for a very tired Clint Adams.

The good news was that he'd come out of that session several hundred dollars richer. The bad news was that word had spread through the small town of Los Gatos, New Mex-ico, about Clint's proficiency with cards, making it harder for him to find any more suitable opponents, no matter how small the stakes.

At half past noon on a weekday, there weren't a lot of people at the Dead Palmer Saloon besides himself, the bar-tender and a pair of bored dealers. Too wide awake to head back to his hotel room, Clint decided to stay in the saloon until he lost some of the wind in his sails. After a winning streak like the one he'd had, such a task was far easier said than done.

1

Pete, the skinny young Navajo dealer who wore his thick black hair pulled into a tail that reached halfway down his back, shifted in his seat and let out a tired breath. "You about ready for breakfast yet?"

Clint had eight showing and a deuce in his hand. "It's closer to lunchtime, and no, I'm not ready to stop. Hit me."

The Indian tossed the Jack of Clubs in front of Clint. "I'll be damned if you don't fall over any second, Mister Jenks."

In the hope of having an uneventful stay in Los Gatos, Clint had assumed the name of Marcus Jenks. It was nice to spend a little time away from everything that came along with being the Gunsmith . . . if only for a matter of hours. "I'm a long way from falling over, Pete," Clint said as he set his card down and passed his hand over it to signal that he was staying. "I'm even feeling lucky enough to up the stakes a bit from our normal fifty cents a hand."

Pete shrugged dramatically. "I'm surprised you've been betting so low after the night you've had. What's more to your liking?"

"I win this hand, and my lunch in on the house."

"And if you lose?"

Putting on a look of mild confusion, Clint said, "Lose? I'm sorry. I don't understand the meaning of that word."

The dealer rolled his eyes at the sound of a hearty chuckle coming from the man tending bar. He suppressed the urge to say anything else and instead turned his attention to his cards. There was a six facing up and when he flipped over his second card, he revealed a seven. Ignoring the growing smirk on Clint's face, he tossed out a third card, which was the Queen of Diamonds.

Clint smacked his hands together and rubbed them vigorously. "I'll take a nice thick steak, baked potato, some corn bread and a tall mug of beer."

The bartender, a short, muscular bald man with a waxed handlebar mustache, looked sternly across the room at the dealer. "That meal's coming outta your pocket, Petey."

The Indian was too busy cashing in Clint's chips to notice the playful wink given from the bartender. Clint had gotten to know the man behind the bar pretty well over the last day and a half, even though most of his drinks had been mostly water or coffee. Now that the gambling was over for the moment, Clint got up and stood next to the long wooden bar.

"Hey Al," Clint said to the barkeep, "since this is on the kid, why don't you make that two steaks. And what've you got for dessert?"

Al tugged on his mustache and filled a mug full of beer. "Better not do that, on account of the kid probably won't be able to cover it."

"Huh?" Pete grunted.

"Anyone who loses me money gets thrown into the street, kid. You know that." Al stood behind the bar, glaring over Clint's beer. Sliding the mug into Clint's waiting hand, he was unable to keep his straight face any longer. As soon as he busted into laughter, everyone in the saloon followed suit.

"Better pull that jaw back up, Petey," Al said good-naturedly. "You might let some flies in."

The dealer got up and walked toward the kitchen through a door behind the bar. "To hell with all of ya. I'll be back in a little while."

Although the beer was flat and tasted slightly coppery, it was more than enough to keep Clint's spirits riding high. The substandard brew went down easy enough and he'd had a lot worse in his time. "Here," he said as he tossed a few of the dollars he'd won after less than an hour of blackjack onto the bar. "Put that toward my bill as well as the kid's. Make sure he gets full of something else besides the grief you've been handing him all night."

"Will do, Mister Jenks. I'll get the missus started on those steaks."

Clint nursed the rest of his beer until a full plate of food was set down in front of him. Judging by the smell that rode up on the steam coming from the steak and potato, the food at the Dead Palmer was a hell of a lot better than its beer. Before he got fork and knife in hand, a bowl covered in a linen napkin was put next to the plate. Inside of that was a golden chunk of corn bread.

Clint was soon joined by the dealer who stood at the bar with his head hung low and a somber look on his face. That look was replaced by sheer confusion when Al tossed a plate identical to Clint's onto the bar in front of him. "There you go," the barkeep said. "Try not to let anyone win that off you as well."

The rich brown color of Pete's face became tinted with red and he dug into the delicious meal. "Like I said before. To hell with all of you."

"Meal's on Mister Jenks," Al added.

Pete turned toward Clint. "Uhh . . . I mean everyone except for you, sir."

"Thanks for clearing that up," Clint said between bites. "I might have lost some sleep over that one."

Once again, Al, the barkeep, busted out into laughter.

Clint didn't bother taking his plate to one of the nearby tables. Actually, it felt rather good being on his feet and filling his stomach with a home-cooked meal. A warm breeze drifted in through the front doors, which had been propped open by an empty keg, and the heat brushed over Clint's neck like a woman's lips.

He was feeling so good that he nearly forgot about the Colt hanging at his side. For the last few days, life had been too quiet to think of the gun as anything but extra weight on his hip. The modified Colt was sporting some newly acquired parts after being repaired not too long ago and since then, he'd been too busy relaxing to concern himself with shooting anybody.

That good feeling lasted right up to the moment when gunshots rang out from the street just beyond the saloon's front door.

TWO

Even though the shots weren't being aimed in his direction, Clint's first reaction was to go for his Colt and dive into the fray. Before he got a chance to think twice about what he was doing, he realized his hand was already touching the smooth wood grain of the pistol's handle.

The bartender appeared from the back room wearing an expression of angry annoyance. "Damn fools come through here every month shooting up the place as though they own the whole blasted town. Don't let 'em get to ya, Mister Jenks."

Clint didn't even bother trying to hide the deadly glint that had turned his eyes into steely slits. "Who are *they*?"

Already on his way around the bar, Al mumbled in a gruff, scratchy voice to himself while picking up a shotgun that had been previously hidden beneath the wooden countertop. He didn't even hear Clint's question as he stepped up to the front door and stuck his head outside, making sure to keep the shotgun hidden behind the door's frame.

With the door open, Clint could hear the sounds of horses riding toward the saloon, their hooves pounding against the clay-packed ground like primal fists beating against the side of a drum. A few more shots rang out, this time followed by voices screaming wildly down the street.

Clint didn't need to see the riders' faces to picture the wide, bloodshot eyes turned up toward the sky and the hands

5

whipping over their heads. Whoever it was making all the racket sounded as though they were having one hell of a celebration and they didn't care one bit who knew about it.

Al's knuckles whitened around the shotgun as the sounds drew closer, but in a matter of seconds, the screaming and hoof beats faded away. It took a bit longer, but eventually the gunshots became nothing more than sharp ripples in the afternoon air.

The barkeep snorted distastefully as he pulled himself back inside the saloon and strode around the bar as though he'd been the one to drive the revelers away. "They'll be back later tonight, I'm sure," he said as he stuffed the shotgun back into its hiding place. "Looks like they're gone for now, though. Sorry about that, Mister Jenks. Just a bunch of rowdies is all."

Feeling the muscles in his shoulders loosen up, Clint became aware that his hand was wrapped around the Colt's grip. He released the pistol and looked down at the remainder of his lunch. "You get a lot of that type around here?"

"Some times more than others. There's ranchers that drive their herds up north in the spring and when those cowboys come through, this place gets a lot noisier."

"That wasn't a bunch of cowboys," Clint pointed out. "In fact, it only sounded like two or three riders, tops. More than that, it sounded as though you knew who they were before you even grabbed that shotgun."

Al glanced from the bar to the door and then back at Clint. A single bead of sweat pushed its way out of his clean-shaven scalp and traced a glimmering line down his face. Wiping it away with a swipe of his hand, the barkeep shrugged and said, "I had my notions."

"You get a lot of notions that cause you to grab for a gun before doing anything else?"

"I wasn't the only one going for their gun, mister. Were you expecting trouble?"

Clint shifted in his spot and tore off another hunk of corn bread. "I'm not trying to start anything with you. Just asking questions, that's all."

"Aw, hell," Al said as he reached for Clint's mug and

topped it off. "Sorry about that. I tend to get a bit jumpy whenever I catch word that Kinman might be headed back this way. Guess I shoulda warned you about that."

"Who's Kinman?" Clint asked. "Some kind of local trouble?"

The young Navajo to Clint's right grumbled while sawing off a piece of his steak. "Trouble don't begin to cover it. Kinman wouldn't be so much trouble if we had a sheriff that was worth a damn."

"That'll be enough of that, Petey," Al scolded. Turning to Clint, the barkeep waved away the dealer's words as though they were nothing more than flies buzzing around the younger man's head. "We got some fine law around here, Mister Jenks. Don't let nobody tell you any different."

At first, Clint was confused by the barkeep's sudden change in attitude. Al had gone from fighting mad to peacekeeper in the blink of an eye. But when the front door swung open and slammed against the wall, the answer presented itself in the form of a bearded Mexican wearing a badge pinned to his chest. It seemed that Al's hearing was even sharper than his tongue.

"Evenin'," the sheriff muttered as he walked in and pulled out a chair at one of the tables at the back of the room.

Clint didn't let a second pass by before he turned around and tipped his hat to the lawman. "I don't suppose you heard that commotion a minute ago, Sheriff?"

"Sure did. Have to be deaf to miss that."

"True enough. Was it your deputies that rode them away from here?"

"Nah," the sheriff grunted. "No need to bother them. Kinman don't stir up too much ruckus before moving on. Besides, Kinman ain't the biggest problem in this town anyway. Not when we got so many dirty redskins draggin' their carcasses along our streets."

Next to Clint, the young Navajo tensed. His lips were drawn tight against his skull to reveal a glimpse of gnashed teeth just below the surface. Al put out a steadying hand and shook his head. It was obvious even to Clint that this particular exchange had happened several times before and that the dealer was getting close to making a bad decision in dealing with the sheriff.

Clint stepped away from the bar, making sure to put himself between Pete and the lawman. "I admit I'm new around here, but doesn't it bother you having someone come riding through your town shooting the place up? Just who is this Kinman that he gets such special treatment?"

"Kinman drinks too much and gets loud sometimes," the sheriff responded. "That's all. I got some disgruntled reports about a certain fella in this very saloon who cleaned out three or four of our town's citizens. You think I should act on those as well?"

"Only if you see someone breaking the law."

Clint was now standing at the sheriff's table, looking down at the lawman. Even though there was nothing worth fighting over, Clint had the distinct feeling that he was within inches of a distinctly unpleasant encounter. The sheriff struck him as so many others had in so many different towns. It was too early to say if the lawman was corrupt, but he was definitely a bully—a trait that wasn't uncommon in those with similar power.

All this time, the sheriff had yet to look into Clint's eyes. Instead, the bearded Mexican had been concentrating on the drink that had been set in front of him. He stared down into that glass of liquor as though it had the ability to look back. "How about you concern yourself with your cards and I'll worry about Kinman." Now, the sheriff did look up. "That agreeable to you, mister?"

There was a definite edge to the sheriff's voice, which shone through like the fangs in a coyote's smile. It was a not-too-subtle warning for Clint to back away and be quick about it.

With no real reason to push the man any further, Clint pretended to be affected by the lawman's words and backed away. "I'm not here for any trouble," he said.

Holding Clint's gaze, the sheriff said, "Good, because trouble is what Kinman is all about."

THREE

With the Dead Palmer being such a small saloon, there wasn't anyplace in there where Clint could talk without being overheard by everyone else. Mostly, it was the sheriff that concerned him since he was the man that he wanted to ask the others about.

The lawman didn't seem interested in spending any more time in the place than what was needed to scarf down his food and toss back a few drinks. In less than half an hour, the potbellied lawman got up from his seat and left the saloon without even checking to see whether or not Al had dropped off a bill.

In that short span of time, two other gamblers had wandered into the saloon with money in their pockets and high hopes obviously drifting inside their minds. Clint had positioned himself to watch the sheriff just in case anything happened that was worth seeing. Besides chewing and lifting the glass to his face, the sheriff barely moved much at all in the hour or two the game lasted. Once the sheriff left, Clint cashed out and excused himself from the game.

"Done already?" Al asked as Clint walked up to the bar.

"Guess I'm finally losing some of my steam. Besides, I've been meaning to ask you a few things."

Besides the other card players, only one other patron had found his way into the place, and that was an old man who

9

sat with his nose almost buried in a mug half full of beer. Al made sure that the old man was appeased for the moment before turning back toward Clint. "Ask away," he said.

Clint looked around to check if anyone was taking an interest in what he was doing. As far as he could tell, nobody seemed to care much about anything else beyond their cards or their drinks. "How's that sheriff of yours? Seems like a decent sort."

"Sheriff Montez?" Al asked as though he was making sure that he and Clint were thinking about the same person. "You'd be one of the few to put it like that, but I'd have to agree with you." Leaning in a little closer, he added, "Doesn't have any love for the Injuns, though, I can tell you that much."

"Yeah. I noticed. Has he ever acted on that?"

"Acted on it?" Al said, while furrowing his brow. "Not anything more than a few nasty words. I try to keep Petey in line because I don't want to see him get into any trouble, but Sheriff Montez wouldn't do anything too bad to the kid."

Clint thought of himself as a good judge of character, which was something he'd earned after years of being out among his fellow men. There was nothing about the way the barkeep acted or talked to make him think Al was lying, but there was still something about what had happened earlier that just didn't sit right with him. "Then why did I get the feeling that the sheriff was trying to provoke Pete into starting something? Does he always treat the people in town like that?"

"He's got a tough job, Mister Jenks. It takes a certain kind of man to do what he does for a living."

"I've met men that are a lot of different types. A lot of them are the kind I'd never like to see again."

Al shook his head and started nervously cleaning the top of the bar. "Sheriff Montez ain't like that. He's all talk." A cloud seemed to pass over his face just then, almost as though he'd been reminded of something that was better off left where it had been buried. "In a way, things might be better around here if he was a little quicker to pull that gun of his."

Nodding, Clint said, "You're talking about Kinman, right?"

"Kinman and . . . there are others."

"Outlaws?"

"Pretty much, but they don't spend all their time around here. They seem to prefer robbing smaller towns with no law at all. That doesn't stop them from rolling through here and taking what they can when they can get it. But Kinman's bunch seems to drift through here more'n the others . . . especially lately."

"Others?"

"There's another gang that's usually on Kinman's heels. They camp outside of town lately, but they're dogs just like the others and come to pick some of the meat off of folks when they get hungry enough. From what I hear, they don't stray too far from their territory." Wiping at the countertop while shaking his head, Al muttered, "Dogs, I tell ya."

"How far out does their territory go?"

Al kept wiping dust off the top of the bar as he turned a more careful eye toward Clint. "You're asking an awful lot of questions, Mister Jenks. You sound like you might be trying to learn something besides what you're asking. It might help if you just come right out and say what's on your mind."

"All right," Clint said. "Is Sheriff Montez on the side of the law or does he get his money from the richer element around here?"

Al didn't seem at all surprised by the question. In fact, he looked as though that had been exactly what he'd been expecting the entire time. "Montez is too lazy to work with them bandits. If he did that, he might actually have to get up off his backside and put in some work. He may not look it, mister, but he's an honest lawman. Lazy, but honest."

Clint let the barkeep's words linger in the air for a bit before they finally faded away with the rest of the saloon's background noise. More people were starting to make their way into the place and all but a few of the spots at the card tables were filling up. Whether his suspicions had been satisfied or he was just losing interest in them, Clint couldn't tell. All he did know was that his questions seemed to be going nowhere, the cards were calling out to him and he still felt some life in his lucky streak.

After downing the rest of his beer, Clint set his mug on the bar. "I'll take your word for it, Al. Hell, as long as I've got a place to play poker right now, I can't really complain too much."

"You heading back for another stretch of stealin' people's hard-earned money?"

"Just a little one."

"But you didn't ask the one question I thought would be on the tip of yer tongue."

"Which one's that?"

"The one about Kinman, of course. Usually, folks hear about an outlaw like that riding so close to where they're sittin' and they can barely contain themselves."

"I guess I've seen more than my share of outlaws. Besides, why do I have to worry about outlaws with a fine, upstanding lawman like Sheriff Montez around?"

Al didn't even try to hide the smirk on his face. At that moment, Pete had emerged from the back room and was headed for his station at the blackjack table. He wore his anger like a set of worn clothing that, even though it was dirty and not too good to look at, seemed to fit him well enough.

Clint was about to sit down at the blackjack table when he saw the anger building on Pete's face. He knew that talking to the Navajo would have gotten him nothing more than a steady stream of curses aimed at the sheriff. Instead, Clint went back to his poker table and kept one ear open for the sound of hoof beats and gunshots coming from outside.

They came before he could finish his third hand.

FOUR

They came like a thunderstorm creeping in from the other side of a mountain range. The gunshots were distant at first, blocked by the buildings of Los Gatos. But as the horses carried their riders closer, they echoed down the street and blasted away the silence that had settled in after they'd come through the first time. This time, however, they didn't just pass by. Instead, the hooves stomped outside the saloon and stayed there. When they stopped, the sound of the horses' panting voices tore through the air.

Al was already coming from around the bar, his shotgun gripped in both hands. "Why does Kinman have ta come here every damn time?"

Just then, the door slammed open and nearly knocked the barkeep off his feet. "Because you serve the only beer in this town that doesn't make me retch," came a voice from outside.

Clint swiveled in his chair, ready to take action if he was needed. All he could see was the large frame of a man standing in the doorway. It had to have been that one who'd kicked in the door. Now, he just stood there glaring down at Al as if he was about to squash him beneath his boot.

The man must have been close to six and a half feet tall. When he took another step inside, Clint could see the giant was wearing a leather vest with no shirt underneath. Thick scars tore up and down his massive arms, creating a pale spiderweb design, which looked even paler in comparison to his darkly tanned skin. A thick mane of coal-black hair hung down past his shoulders. The hulking figure wore a machete strapped to his side where anyone else might carry a gun. Clint couldn't see the man's other side, but would have placed his bet on the pistol being there.

"You gonna do somethin', Con?" Al asked defiantly. "Or are you just gonna take up space in my doorway?"

"I paid you a compliment," came that same voice from before. "Now how about a drink for me and my men?"

The fact that the giant's lips didn't move seemed odd to Clint. But then Con took a step to one side and cleared the way for the person who'd been doing the talking. The figure that walked in next was a much better fit for the spirited, almost melodic voice that had come before.

Clint looked at the other men sitting at his table. "Who is that?" he asked to the man on his left.

"That's Andy Kinman."

"I thought Al called him Con."

"Con's the big fella. Andy's the one behind him."

Clint turned back toward the front door and took another look at Andy Kinman. After all he'd heard about the outlaw and after seeing Al's quickness to pull a shotgun on the man, Clint hadn't been exactly sure what to expect. One thing for sure, he certainly wasn't expecting Kinman to be a woman.

She stood about a foot shorter than Con. Wearing a light brown duster and dirty leather boots, she looked every bit of the role she was playing, right down to the double-rig holster that could be seen when she opened her coat to set her hands upon her hips. With a swipe of her hand, she tossed back the battered hat that had been on top of her head and let it hang by a chin strap to reveal tousled light brown hair that had been in the sun enough for it to acquire blonde streaks running all the way through. Her full, red lips were turned up in a mischievous smile that sent a shimmer all the way up into her rich brown eyes.

"Put that thing away, Al, before you hurt someone," she

said to the barkeep. Andy walked past Al and swatted the shotgun aside as though it was a child's toy. When she got to the bar, she pounded on its surface with a calloused fist, which started a stream of rough-looking men to come in through the door.

"I told you the last time, Kinman," Al snarled. "You can't come in here every few weeks and take apart my saloon. How am I supposed to make a living if I'm always fixing the holes you blow through my walls?"

"That's why I made sure to do all my shooting outside. But I'll be glad to make an exception," she said while spinning around to glare at everyone else in the place, "if any of these people decide to collect on the price that's on my head."

Although the look in her eyes wasn't particularly threatening, it was obvious that one word from the woman would turn her men loose like a pack of wild dogs. Con, in particular, seemed anxious to be unleashed.

"No takers?" she asked. When none of the people in the saloon spoke up, Kinman nodded her head and smiled with genuine warmth. "Good. Then y'all can get back to what you were doing and just pretend we're not even here."

Besides the fact that he seemed more happy with the notion of taking the chance of getting his head blown off rather than put up with Kinman and her group, Al seemed to be doing all right. He allowed himself to be pushed aside and eventually took shelter behind the bar as man after man came swaggering into his saloon.

Clint watched all of this with growing amusement. There were ten men in total, not counting Con and their leader. Kinman seemed to be making herself at home, slapping the rugged outlaws on their backs and snatching a shot glass from the bar as soon as it had been filled.

She stopped what she was doing at one point so she could look over the faces of the crowd. When her eyes met each of them in turn, the locals would quickly face another direction or even avert their gaze to the ceiling or floor rather than stare back at the outlaw leader. But when her eyes found Clint's, Andy's locked on and stayed there.

He was the only one who didn't turn away from her. And he was the only one who didn't seem uncomfortable being in the crowded saloon.

Andy stepped over to Con, who was standing near the blackjack table, and slapped the giant on his shoulder. Pulling on his vest as though she was trying to tear it off of him, she got the big man to bend down so she could put her mouth close to his ear. She said something to him that made him turn to glance over at Clint with the same look in his eyes that a hungry wolf might give to a limping prairie dog.

Clint couldn't tell what was being said, but he kept a confident look on his face all the same. Con glared back at him and then turned away, shaking his head while saying something back to Andy. She listened and they both exchanged knowing glances before Andy started pushing her way through her men, digging out a path that led straight to Clint's table.

"Mind if I sit in?" she asked once she finally got to the spot directly across from Clint.

FIVE

There was already an older gentleman sitting in that chair, but after a pat on the shoulder from Andy, he got to his feet and relinquished his spot. In fact, the gray-haired man seemed relieved to be excused.

Clint tipped his hat to the outlaw and nodded. "Always a pleasure to play cards with a lady. I'll take all the good luck I can get."

"Well, I believe that's the first time I've ever been called that," she said while sitting down.

"All ladies are good luck."

"I meant that's the first time I've ever been called a lady."

When Andy slipped out of her duster and pulled her hair straight back and out of her face, she looked less like the leader of a group of outlaws and more like a beautiful young woman. By the looks of it, she was somewhere in her late twenties. Beneath the long coat, she wore a loosely buttoned man's shirt that was unable to hide the shapely curves of her firm, round breasts.

She glanced around the table at all the others sitting behind their stacks of chips. "How much to buy in?" she asked.

Clint was shuffling and was also the banker since most

of the chips on the table belonged to him. "Five dollars.
It's just a friendly little game."

Reaching into her shirt pocket, she pulled out a few rumpled bills and tossed them onto the table. "I'll take however
many that buys me."

Clint counted the money and gave her chips for the
amount of seven dollars. He then waited for everyone to
throw in their ante and dealt the cards. Despite the noise in
the place, there wasn't much going on inside the Dead
Palmer that shouldn't be expected in any other saloon.
Some of Andy's men got out of hand, but they were mostly
picking fights with each other. Even so, there wasn't anything beyond a mild scuffle to worry about.

For the most part, it was just a large group of men gathered around a little bar, doing their best to get drunk as
quickly as humanly possible. Once Andy got a drink in
front of her and some cards in her hand, she blended in
with all the other players, making pleasant conversation and
winning no more than the odds should allow. In fact,
Clint's luck was still holding out.

He was reaching across the table to pull in his most recent pile of winnings when he looked over at Andy. She
was looking right back at him, just as she'd been doing for
the last hour and a half.

"You never told me your name," she said.

"You never asked."

"Well, I'm asking right now."

Clint knew that anyone who ran in circles that respected
skill with a gun would recognize his name almost immediately. His mind raced in two directions, wondering if he
should own up to his true identity or see what would happen if he could be seen as just another face in the crowd.
"It's Marcus Jenks. You're Andy Kinman?"

She gave a little laugh and took the deck of cards as they
were handed off to her. "I suppose Al yelled that out loud
enough for the folks in Tucson to hear my name. It's short
for Andrea."

"I guessed as much."

"You're a hell of a poker player. I haven't seen you around here before. Just passing through?"

"Pretty much," Clint said with a nod. "Enjoying the cards and quiet atmosphere. Well . . . the cards anyway."

Smiling in a way that just tugged slightly at the corners of her mouth, Andy dealt the cards and set the rest of the deck onto the table beside her drink. "Me and my men were passing through as well. Didn't see any harm in stopping by for a drink and some gambling. After all, this is a saloon, right?"

Clint raised his hands slightly. "I'm not trying to start anything. Just speaking my mind."

All the while, the others at the table had been keeping their noses in their cards and their comments to themselves. Although they seemed to have relaxed somewhat since Andy's dramatic entrance, they didn't seem ready to kick back and shoot the bull with her, either. Instead, they played their hands, drank their drinks and let Clint and Andy do all the talking.

Andy kept smiling at Clint and played through the hand, winning with a straight flush. "Guess maybe I'm a lucky lady after all," she said slyly.

She started to lean forward as if to say something else to Clint, but was cut off as the front door to the saloon flew open and a man dressed in dirty riding gear came storming through. Recognizing the man immediately, Andy threw down her cards and jumped to her feet.

"What is it, Jack?" she asked once the man had spotted her and rushed forward.

Sucking in his breaths with great, gasping wheezes, the new arrival had more than likely run from his horse up to the bar, if not all the way around the block a few times. "I just . . . just got word back from the border. Pearson knows about our next job and is riding down there to beat us to the punch."

SIX

"What?" Andy snarled as all vestiges of her calm demeanor were replaced by a mask of sheer rage. "How the hell did Pearson find out where we were headed?"

"Damned if I know. I got ahold of one'a their gang and he told me what was going on."

"Are you sure the guy wasn't lying? He could've been trying to throw you off the trail."

"Not after what I did to him. *Nobody's* men are that loyal."

Andy's first response was to grab for the pistol that hung at her side. Rather than draw the weapon, however, she clenched her fist around it and stormed over to the big man who was still leaning against the blackjack table. Clint couldn't hear what she said, but when Con slammed his fist through the wooden planks, it was easy enough to figure out the gist of what Andy had told him.

"Come on," Andy said to the men that had gathered around her. "We ride now! That money's still ours and if we have to kill all of Pearson's men to get it, then that's just what we'll do."

All of the outlaws gave a snarling battle cry as they began pouring out of the saloon. Andy let them all go before turning to look back at Clint.

"We'll have to finish our game later, Marcus," she said. "Just so long as my luck holds out, that is."

Although Clint had been starting to enjoy his game with Andy Kinman, he was happy enough to watch her go. There was something about what he'd heard that just didn't seem to sit right with him. Looking around the saloon, Clint could see that every one of Andy's men had cleared out. Every one . . . except for the one that had been the bearer of the bad news. That one stood away from the door as though he was hoping to be looked over in the midst of all the commotion he'd caused. And besides that, he suddenly didn't seem as tired as he'd been only seconds before.

Clint got to his feet and walked straight for that man. The instant he was spotted, Clint could tell the rough-looking figure was about to make a run for it.

"Sounds like an awfully big stroke of luck for you to get your hands on one of Pearson's men like that," Clint said.

"Who the hell are you?" the man grunted.

"Someone who should probably keep his eyes closed and mouth shut more often. Unfortunately, I just can't seem to walk away when someone's about to ride into a bloodbath."

The man's eyes narrowed and he took another couple of steps toward the door. "You'd do well to follow yer own advice, mister."

"As far as I can tell, there's only one problem with the story you gave to Miss Kinman." Clint didn't even wait for the man to reply. Instead, he walked toward the suddenly nervous man and said, "You see, I know all about Pearson. At least, I've heard an awful lot about the way Pearson's gang works and one of the first things I heard was that those fellas tend to travel in packs. If you got your hands on one of them, then you would have had to fight your way through a hell of a lot more than that."

Walking up a bit closer, Clint slowly eyed the man up and down. "I don't even see a scratch on you."

"Maybe I got lucky."

"Sure . . . or maybe you're lying."

Despite all the parts of Clint's brain that screamed at him to back off and tend to his own affairs, it was simply too

late for him to do so. Outlaws or no, Kinman and her men
didn't deserve to get slaughtered by riding headfirst into a
storm of lead. Clint knew it would be a bad idea to sit back
and let the fireworks go unchecked.

Besides, nobody deserved to be slaughtered.

If anything, outlaws deserved to meet their justice the
way everyone else did; through a judge and jury. The man
in front of Clint was lying. Clint was sure of it now. All
he needed was one more bit of proof to be positive.

"Stand aside," the man said with a thick layer of bravado.
"You've wasted enough of my time with this bullshit."

"The only way you could've met up with less than four
of Pearson's men would be if you caught Pearson himself.
He rides with one other man from time to time."

"That's right."

"So you managed to fight off Pearson and get ahold of
that one man?"

"Yeah, so I suggest you let me pass before I put you
down just like I did to that one other man."

"Pearson's a tough man," Clint said, studying the liar's
face. "And you beat him all by yourself?"

There was no twinge in the other man's features. Besides
the intent, threatening glare in his eyes, there was only the
obvious desire to get the hell out of that saloon. "You heard
what I said. I got around him long enough to get ahold of
his guard," he said as his hand went for his gun. "Now get
the hell out of my way before I put a hole through your
skull."

Clint stepped aside, knowing full well that his suspicions
had been confirmed. There was no doubt in his mind about
the other man now. He was lying. That meant that he'd
also been lying to Kinman.

Normally, Clint didn't take to protecting the lawless, but
when two rival gangs fought, there was more than enough
violence to spill over onto the innocents who happened to
be too close to the war zone. The only thing worse than a
gang at war was when one of those gangs managed to win.
Usually, the victors were never happy for very long and
when strong, victorious gangs got restless, that meant even

more trouble for whoever they happened to see. Clint knew he was standing in one of the first towns that would be hit by the fallout.

And that, most definitely, was something he could not let happen.

"There's one big problem with your story," Clint said once the other man had passed and was about to open the saloon's front door.

That man didn't turn around. Instead, his body tensed and he tightened his grip on the handle of his gun. "What's that?" he snarled.

"Pearson isn't a tough man at all. Pearson doesn't like to be seen by his enemies. And before you tell me all about your masterful tracking skills, I'll tell you one thing that Pearson has in common with your Kinman . . . they're both women."

Knowing his lie was out there for all to see, the man swore beneath his breath and took the only path that was left open to him. He spun around while drawing his gun, filling the saloon's air with smoky explosions and lead.

SEVEN

Clint could see the shot coming as though it had been fired through a vat of molasses, allowing plenty of time for Clint to throw his body down to the side as the chunk of lead whipped over his head.

The people remaining inside the saloon followed suit and dove for cover beneath tables or behind any piece of furniture that was big enough. Laying with his face pressed against the uneven planks covering the floor, Al reached a careful hand out to grab hold of his shotgun. Once he had the weapon in his grasp, he clicked back the hammers and got ready to fire.

Rolling to the side as soon as he hit the ground, Clint came up on one knee with his modified Colt locked in his fist. He tensed his finger on the trigger, taking the extra half-second to concentrate on his aim. "You get that one for free, boy," Clint said. "Try for another and I'll kill you where you stand."

The words were barely out of Clint's mouth before the gunman turned on the ball of his foot and swung his pistol around to take another shot. The smoke from his first attempt still swirled around his head and stung the corners of his eyes. The bitter taste of gunpowder coated the back of his throat as he pulled back on his trigger and felt the pistol buck one more time in the palm of his hand.

Reading the shooter's eyes was easier to Clint than reading the headlines of the morning paper. Before the other man got his shot off, Clint was rolling one more time to the side, landing in the same spot he'd been standing in only seconds ago. Still on one knee, Clint pointed the Colt as though he was pointing his finger, squeezed the trigger and watched the other man fall.

The liar's face twisted into a contorted mask of pain as Clint's lead tore a fiery hole through his hip. The impact spun him as though he'd been hit with a mining pick and sent him into a tight downward spiral that drove him like a screw into the floor. He landed on both knees with his back to Clint, the warm trickle of blood coursing over his leg.

Clint got back to his feet without moving his aim from the back of the other man's head. Two careful steps brought him close enough to send his left boot into the wounded man's wrist, which sent the liar's gun straight up into the air.

"Sometimes," Clint said as he snatched the gun out of the air with his free hand, "I don't know why I bother trying to give men like you a sporting chance."

The liar was trying to say something, but every time he started to speak, his words were cut off by an agonizing wave of heat spiking from the wound and traveling throughout his entire body. "Wh-why did . . ."

"Why did I call your bluff?" Clint finished. "Or why did I let you live?"

Hearing that, the wounded man seemed to realize for the first time just how close he'd come to meeting his maker. His hand went to the empty holster at his side as though somehow his gun would be there waiting for him. When his last hope was dashed, he lowered his head and waited for the inevitable. "Either," he said.

Clint looked around the saloon and saw that most of the people who'd been hiding themselves were finally screwing up enough courage to poke their heads out from cover and see who was winning the fight. When they saw Clint standing over the second man, a lot of them felt secure enough to get back to their feet and make their way out the back door.

Al rose up from behind the bar with the shotgun held up to his shoulder. "I got your back covered, Mister Jenks."

At first, Clint had forgotten about the name he'd given to the barkeep. But after a second or two, the name struck a chord and he nodded his approval. "Much obliged," he said without taking his eyes away from the wounded man. "But why don't you make sure that everyone else gets out of here rather than worry about me. I can take care of this one just fine."

"Yeah," Al said as he walked around the bar and lowered his gun so he wouldn't be pointing it at Clint. "It looks like you don't need much help at all."

Clint waited for Al to walk past and make his way to the back of the saloon before nudging the wounded man with the barrel of his Colt. "Get up."

"But you shot my leg," the man whined.

"Then get up fast before too much pain sets in. Your comfort isn't my biggest concern right now."

The wounded man gritted his teeth and reached out for Clint to help him up. Rather than extend a hand, Clint kicked over one of the nearby chairs for him to use for support. Taking a step back, Clint let him fight his way to his feet and then drop himself into the chair. Once he was sitting down again, the man sucked in several ragged breaths and let them out as though they burned his throat. Beads of sweat glistened on his brow and dripped down over his face to soak into the collar of his shirt.

"Now start talking," Clint said.

"I need to see a doctor."

"The quicker you tell me what I want to know, the quicker that will happen. Since you were the one that drew on me, I've got no problem with standing here and watching you bleed out."

The man tried to put on a tough face, but the facade was broken as soon as another jolt of pain lanced through his body and caused him to twitch in agony. "What the hell do you want from me?"

"You can start by telling me why you'd want to set up Kinman. From the way she talked to you, I'd say you're part of her gang. Why lie to her?"

"Because she's about to get one of the biggest scores of her life and she's set to keep most of it for herself. The men she rides with only get to split up half of it among all of us." Another spasm of pain rocked through his leg, this time causing him to suck in a pained breath. "Damn bitch needs to stop bein' so greedy."

Clint was still imagining what kind of trap Kinman was riding into. Even though he wanted to catch up to her and keep her from springing it, he knew better than to charge off against unknown odds. "What job are you talking about? How much is it worth?"

For a second, it looked as though the man was going to hold his tongue. Then, he reached down to grab his leg and felt the blood that had completely soaked through his pants and formed a slick, sticky layer extending down past his knee. It was obvious by the look on his face that, although he might have been used to the sight of blood, he was none too happy to see so much of his own. Some more of the color left his cheeks and he began to sway in his seat.

He looked up at Clint and seemed to decide something in his mind. "I never met Pearson, but I got word from his . . . I mean . . . her gang that they would pay good for anyone in Kinman's gang who would hand her over. I heard about the deal we'd be getting and decided to jump the fence. Pearson was paying more anyway."

"More than what?"

"Three hundred thousand dollars in gold and silver."

Clint's poker face had been perfected to the point that it resembled something carved into the side of a mountain. But when he heard that amount, even he was unable to keep from flinching. "Where the hell did she get ahold of that much money?"

"She ain't got it yet, but that's how much is at stake at a tournament being held in Rock Bottom, Arizona. With Kinman out of the picture, I figured I had a better shot at that prize." His features tainted with defeat, the man looked away from Clint and gripped his leg tightly. "I figure if you took me down, then I wouldn't stand much of a chance against you anyways. You *are* on your way to the tournament, right?"

Clint's mind was racing with all this new information. He had no idea what kind of tournament he was talking about or even where on earth Rock Bottom, Arizona, was. But rather than try to figure all of that out now, he decided to worry about the first problem. "Where is Pearson going to ambush Kinman?"

"Andy was gonna take an old prospector's trail leading southwest through Arizona and then down into Mexico. We were headed that way anyway, but I was to make sure they left before they had too much time to rest up."

"And once they were there, you'd be shooting at Kinman's gang instead of Pearson's, right?"

The wounded man nodded. "I don't know anything else but that."

Clint wasn't sure if the other man was holding out on any more information or not and frankly, he didn't have any more time to waste on him. "Stay here," Clint said while heading for the front door. "I'll get a doctor to come for you, but you can be sure of one thing. If I find out you're lying, I'll come back and finish what I started."

"I don't doubt it, mister. I wouldn't have said so much if I thought any different."

Clint left the saloon and launched himself up onto Eclipse's back. The Darley Arabian stallion reared slightly, but only in anticipation of a thundering ride with the wind in his face and the ground flying beneath his hooves.

He wasn't disappointed.

EIGHT

Clint had been counting on the arid New Mexican terrain to be in his favor as he snapped Eclipse's reins and headed off. Sure enough, even after the couple of minutes spent at the saloon after Kinman and her gang had left, there was still some of the cloud of dust remaining that had been kicked up by all the departing horses. It wasn't much, but it was enough to tell Clint that he was 'leaded in the right direction as he bolted down one of the main streets of Los Gatos, which quickly took him out of town.

Once the town was behind him, it was even easier to see which way the gang had gone. The weather was clear and the terrain was flat enough for Clint to see for miles in every direction. Up ahead, he could plainly see the large group of riders traveling southwest, kicking up a dirty cloud in their wake. Clint touched his heels once again to Eclipse's sides and lowered his body down along the stallion's back.

Eclipse broke into a full gallop. The Darley Arabian's hooves only touched the ground briefly before launching the rest of its body into a horizontal flight that carried him over the land like a force of nature rather than just another one of its creatures. He pushed his neck forward and back in perfect rhythm as his hooves stomped into the ground, taking himself and the man on his back even faster toward their destination.

Clint couldn't help but marvel at the way the stallion moved. When the Darley Arabian hit top speed, he seemed to make even less noise than when he was simply walking softly from one point to another. Besides the wind in his ears, all Clint could hear was a steady tapping of hooves against packed earth and the deep bellows of the animal's lungs trading air with the outside world.

Keeping his eyes on the dust cloud up ahead, Clint only had to lightly tug on the reins to adjust Eclipse's aim. He got a better feeling in his gut concerning the location of the ambush, simply because there wasn't much of anything in the area besides the occasional crop of boulders that could be used as a hiding place. That meant that wherever Pearson would be waiting for them, it had to be several miles down the road.

Clint could feel him and Eclipse gaining on Kinman and her group with every step the stallion took. As the dust cloud got steadily closer, he took a bit of time to think about what he was about to do.

As far as he could tell, there was growing hostilities between the gangs led by Kinman and Pearson. He'd heard about Pearson just by keeping his ears open while he was in the area a few years back. Although not much more than a robber at the time, Pearson had been making a good name for herself among outlaws and lawmen alike. A year ago, Clint had heard that she'd been wanted for several bank and stagecoach robberies throughout the southwest.

In fact, she'd become so good at her work that Pearson's name became associated strictly with her deeds rather than the novelty of her being a woman in a man's line of work. Clint had spoken to a sheriff in Nevada who only knew Pearson by that one name, assuming that the robber was a man. At the time, Clint had said nothing, nodded his head and stored away the bit of information for later use.

Since Pearson wasn't in the league of some of the other local legends, her gang had just been lumped in with the rest of the local threats. But now, it seemed as though she was set to make a play for a bigger piece of the action. Clint had never heard of Kinman or her gang until a day or two ago, but it seemed as though she was in direct competition with Pearson. That, at least, was one way that the gangs were exactly like the ones led by men: Both groups still fought over territory like a couple of rabid dogs circling each other and nipping at the other's neck over a freshly killed meal.

Thanks to Eclipse's speed and stamina, they would be closing in on Kinman's gang within minutes. Clint flicked the reins just to stoke the stallion's fires a bit as his mind raced with all the implications of the things he'd learned. First, there was the fight coming between the two gangs that would surely spill over into more than one neighboring town. Then there was the mysterious tournament that the man at the Dead Palmer had referred to. And finally, there was the question of the tournament's main prize: Where had that gold and silver come from? How many others were after it? And what were they all prepared to do to get it?

Clint hated to admit it, but he was curious as hell to find out who was behind a tournament of outlaws and how they'd gotten their hands upon a supply of three hundred thousand dollar's worth of gold and silver. Another prospect that made it impossible for him to resist was the fact that such a prize would surely bring more than just these two groups out into the open. Clint could only imagine who else would show up at such a spectacle for the chance to get their hands on that kind of money.

Whatever the reason was behind this tournament, Clint knew one thing for sure: It would not result in anything good.

The dust clouds were getting even closer now, so Clint let the stallion run until he began to slow down naturally. Having ridden the Darley Arabian for some time now, Clint could feel when the horse was beginning to tire and knew how much energy was left within the massive muscles writhing beneath the flesh drawn taut over its body.

It was at that moment that Clint caught sight of something that made the bottom drop out of his stomach. Looming in the distance like a freshly imagined mirage was a shallow gorge passing through a narrow canyon less than a few miles away. The formation of rocks had been hidden to him by the glare of the sun as well as the lay of the land and now that he could see it, Clint thought only one thing: If he was planning an ambush, that would have been the perfect spot.

Although Clint knew he could be riding into one hell of a trap himself, he knew that there was never much to gain from playing things safe. After all, the most satisfying wins he'd ever had at the poker table had been when he wasn't exactly sure he could beat the others betting against him.

Clint threw his ante into the middle of the table by raising his pistol and firing a round into the air.

NINE

As soon as Andy heard the gunshot echoing through the air behind her, she held up her hand and closed a fist, signaling for the others to stop. She sat tall in her saddle and listened as the sounds of her group's horses faded away. Within a minute, she heard another set of hooves approaching quickly from the trail they'd left behind. Snapping the reins, she brought her horse around to the back of the group and took a look for herself.

Sure enough, there was another rider kicking up enough dust to be seen despite all the grit thrown into the air by her own men. "Con," she shouted over her shoulder, "get back here."

The bulky man drove his gray mare next to Andy and squinted toward the horizon. "Someone's following us?"

"That's what I see, too. The next question is, Who it could be?"

Another one of the gang brought his horse in close to Andy's other side. Sitting in its saddle was a slender man with more wrinkles on his face than his years should have allowed. His face was covered with coarse stubble and his hands looked as if they'd been crafted out of tanned rawhide. With one smooth motion, he pulled a long rifle from the holster hanging from his saddle and set the weapon

across his lap. "I can pick him off from here. All you got
to do is say the word."

"Ease it back a notch, Stamper," Con said with more than
a little annoyance in his voice. "Let's not put a bullet in
someone until we at least know who we're gonna kill."

Stamper was still easing the lever back on his rifle as he
shot a challenging stare at the much bigger man. It wasn't
until Andy herself looked over at him and shook her head
that Stamper dropped the rifle back into its holster and
shifted in his saddle. "Then what do you suppose we should
do? Wait until he gets here so he can take the first shot at
one of us?"

"No," Andy said. "I say you use something besides that
rifle for a change. Don't you have a telescope in there
somewhere?"

Reaching down to the saddlebags hanging toward the
rear of the horse, Stamper fished inside the pouch on the
left side and pulled out a dented metal cylinder that was
covered with chipped flecks of black paint over a copper
surface. He extended the telescope with a flick of his wrist
and put the small end to his eye. "Well . . . whoever he is,
he's riding alone. Don't recognize the face, though."

"Let me see," Andy said while holding out her hand. She
took the telescope and peered through the glass, moving
her head slightly until she had the approaching rider in her
sights. At first, she looked mildly surprised. Then recognition took hold and a slight smile drifted across her face.

"You know who it is?" Con asked.

"I sure do."

Stamper already had the rifle back against his shoulder
and ready to fire. "You ready for me to take my shot, then?"

"No, Stamper," Andy said with a scolding tone. "You
don't get to pick anyone off just yet." Turning to Con, she
added, "It's one of the men from the Dead Palmer."

Con's face twisted up with undisguised suspicion. "Let
me guess. It's one of the fellas you were playing poker
with."

"You got it. Name's Jenks." After taking one more lingering look through the glass, she moved the telescope

away from her eye and collapsed it against her thigh. When she turned to hand it back to its owner, she found Stamper already fidgeting with his rifle.

Stamper took back the spyglass and dropped it into his bag. "Who's this Jenks? And why should we let him get any closer?"

Watching the growing dust cloud and the stallion at its center, Andy imagined that she was still sitting across from that man at the poker table back in Los Gatos. She'd had a feeling about him then, and now that feeling was growing stronger as he rode closer to her. "My guess is that he's got something to say. Otherwise, he wouldn't have warned us the way he did."

"And if you're wrong?" Con asked.

First, she turned to the giant on her right and then to the sniper to her left. "Then you two boys only have to decide which one of you gets to kill him."

Both of the men next to Andy seemed to like that proposition. They settled into their saddles and waited for the man they knew as Marcus Jenks to get close enough so they might be able to make out his true colors.

Clint let Eclipse run himself out of steam until he was close enough to make out the separate figures in Kinman's gang. From what he could see, there were more than a dozen of them. Three of those had separated from the rest and were waiting for him to get closer.

Hopefully, they took his warning shot as nothing more than an attention grabber or else he could very well be in some serious trouble. Clint's luck held out and he was allowed to approach the gang without much in the way of hostilities directed at him.

By the time he felt the Darley Arabian slowing to a trot, Clint was able to make out the figures that were closest to him. Kinman herself wasn't hard to spot and neither was the giant of a man that had been with her at the saloon. The other, skinnier figure on Kinman's other side, however, was an unknown. Although Clint didn't much like unknowns, he figured that he didn't have much of a choice in this situation.

He pulled back on Eclipse's reins and brought the stallion to a halt about twenty feet away from the gang members. Holding up his hands to show he was no longer wielding his gun, Clint waited there for a second to make sure he wasn't about to get shot.

"What brings you out here?" Andy shouted.

Clint slowly lowered his hands. As soon as they dropped close enough to his waist, the sounds of no less than six guns being cocked rattled through the air. He tried to look a little afraid as he once again lifted his arms skyward. "I came because I thought there was something you ought to know."

When Con dropped to the ground from his saddle, Clint swore he could feel a slight tremor rumbling through the ground. The big man's feet planted squarely in the dusty earth and when he approached, a stray breeze got ahold of his duster and whipped it to the side to reveal the modified double rig around his waist. Instead of going for the pistol, Con went for the machete hanging at his other side.

The giant blade sliced through the air as Con closed the distance between himself and Clint in a few giant strides. Placing the tip of the machete against Clint's stomach, Con gave the blade just enough of a twist to send expectant twinges through Clint's system.

"Take that pistol out real slow," Con said in a soft, rumbling growl. "Use two fingers on the handle and hand it over."

TEN

Clint did as he was told, plucking the Colt from his holster and dropping it into Con's outstretched hand. Parting with the weapon was akin to letting someone saw off his right hand, but he knew that all it would take was a quick twist of the bigger man's wrist and Clint's innards would soon see the light of day.

Besides, he was still playing the part of small-time gambler. The main thing he was hoping for was that none of the gang members would look too carefully at that Colt. After all, no small-time gambler had any business carrying firepower of that caliber.

Once he had the gun, Con tossed it over his shoulder so Andy could snatch it out of the air. Clint's stomach knotted up for a second as she took a look at the pistol. But her gaze stayed on the Colt for no more than a few seconds before she stuck it into her saddlebag. Her eyes drifted toward the rifle hanging from Clint's saddle, but then she looked toward Con and Stamper. Convinced that Clint wouldn't be able to make a move before her men could gun him down, Andy relaxed somewhat.

"So, what brings you out here in such a hurry?" she asked. "By the looks of that horse you're on, you ran it pretty hard to catch up to us."

Clint ran a hand through Eclipse's mane and scratched

37

the stallion behind its ears. "He was due for a good haul. Gets his blood flowing."

Just then, Stamper's hand came up, bringing the rifle to bear on Clint. "I'll get *your* blood flowing if you don't start answering her questions."

Fighting back the urge to stare the rifleman down, Clint kept his innocent look about him and lowered his head. "After you left, the man who told you to come out here said something to one of the other fellas in the saloon."

Con shifted in his saddle and scanned the rest of the gang. When he came up one man short, he turned around to level a stare at Clint that would have been nearly enough to make a rattlesnake think twice about coming any closer. "Where the hell is Zachary?" Pushing the machete a little farther into Clint's flesh, he said, "You got two seconds, boy, before I slice you wide open."

"I heard him talking to this other man at the saloon," Clint said. "They were talking about making sure the others had a chance to get in place before you got to them. He mentioned something about getting paid for all his trouble and that he would be going away as soon as he could slip apart from the rest of you."

"Is that it?" Andy asked.

"He also lied to you," Clint added, making sure to be ready to watch the faces of every one of the gang members that he could see. "I know for a fact he was joining up with Pearson's bunch."

It didn't take much to notice the change that swept over every single one of their expressions. Of the three, Stamper was the one who tipped his hand the most. His eyes went wide and his jaw dropped open in a way that reminded Clint of a starving animal that had just spotted the weakest member of a herd. His fists clenched around his rifle until the knuckles went white.

Con's entire visage turned to stone. Gnashing his teeth together hard enough to make the muscles in his jaw stand out, the big man reflexively moved the machete across Clint's stomach as though he was already thinking about how he would eviscerate the person he was thinking about.

As for Kinman, she looked different as well, but not in the same way as her men. Rather than display blind anger or hostility, she leaned back in her saddle and looked down the trail in the direction of Los Gatos. There was no joy or even any maliciousness in her smile anymore. In fact, it was hard even for Clint to read her expression. One moment, she looked glad to hear Pearson's name and the next, she looked about ready to launch into a rage. Her full lips drew tightly together before parting once again.

"You sure about that?" she asked.

Clint squirmed against the pressure of Con's machete. At that moment, the discomfort he displayed was anything but a performance. "I wouldn't come all this way just to lie to you. I may not know a lot about . . . what you do," Clint said, "but I'm a good judge of character and I make my living from knowing when somebody's bluffing. There was something about the way he spoke to you when he ran into the saloon. If I had to put money on it, I'd say he even sounded desperate to get you out of there and on your way.

"I may have been getting my sounds mixed up, but I thought I also heard him mention something about some kind of tournament. After he said that, he looked over and saw that I was paying a little too much attention to him. That's when everything started getting bad."

Con eased up on the machete a little bit and glanced over his shoulder. Looking back at Clint, he asked, "What do you mean by *bad*?"

"Well . . . that was when he started coming after me, asking about how much I heard and who the hell I was. I told him that maybe you folks should know about what he was saying and then he told me I'd never make it out of that saloon alive. He drew his gun and . . ." Clint let the sentence trail off as he turned so that he wasn't looking at Con.

"Let me guess," Stamper said. "You shot him down."

"Didn't have a choice," Clint said. "It was either that or get used to the notion of being dead."

Andy swung down from her horse and walked between Con and Stamper. She put out her hand and rubbed Eclipse on the muzzle. "That's a hard thing to get used to," she said earnestly. Turning to Con, she motioned for the big man to follow her. To Stamper, she said, "If he tries to make a move, you can kill him." Then she and the bigger man were moving away from the rest.

The glare on Stamper's face turned into a bloodthirsty sneer. He swung the rifle across one knee so that it was aimed at Clint's chest. For a second, it looked as though he was considering pulling the trigger and making up an excuse after the body fell. But Andy and Con didn't take long enough for the rifleman to make up his mind.

Once again, Andy stepped right up to Clint's side and ran her hands over Eclipse. "The only thing keeping you alive," she said, "is that the man you're talking about hasn't been acting right for the better part of a month. In fact, this sounds like just the sort of thing that I was waiting for him to pull."

Kicking Clint's foot from the stirrup so she could climb up and put her lips close to his ear, she whispered just loud enough for him to hear. Her breath was like a warm caress over his skin. "But don't think for one minute that I trust you," she said softly. "I'll be watching you so close, you won't be able to blink your eyes without me knowing about it."

"Doesn't sound too bad," Clint replied. "In fact, the thought of having you close sounds downright desirable."

"You play your cards right and I might get even closer. I find out that you're playing straight and really did go through all this trouble to help me out and you might just come out on top of this whole thing." The corners of her mouth turned up slightly and her tongue flicked out to take a quick taste of Clint's earlobe.

"I do enjoy being on top."

"Top, bottom, standing up or from behind, you'll love every angle you can think of so long as I can trust you."

Clint flashed her a sly grin that was one part challenge and two parts lust. "From what I heard, there's a lot to be gained from this tournament you're going to."

"Oh you know about that as well, do you?" Andy was

leaning back now, locking her eyes onto his before looking him slowly up and down. "How much did he tell you it was worth?"

"Three hundred thousand."

The smile on Andy's face got even bigger, giving her the appearance of a scheming little devil who wasn't even trying to hide the fact of what she was. After dropping back down onto the ground, she moved a hand over Eclipse's coat and then dragged it seductively over Clint's thigh. "That," she said, "is one of the reasons that Zachary has been itching to get out of this gang. I never trusted that son of a bitch. Not even enough to tell him how much money we made."

"Why's that?"

"Because then he wouldn't know how much I was holding back from him."

"So you believe me?" Clint asked.

"About Zachary setting me up for a bullet? Of course. I'm surprised it took him this long to make a move. But as for the rest of it . . . I'm still not sure."

Andy turned her back on Clint and walked over to Stamper. "Keep an eye on him," she said. "Don't make him too uncomfortable, but don't let him get too relaxed either. And if you see him doing anything suspicious . . ."

The rifleman's eyes started to gleam with anticipation.

Jabbing him with her finger for emphasis, Andy said, "Tell me about it before you do anything. If he was able to get the drop on Zachary, then maybe we can use him."

"To hell with that," Stamper spat. "I'll bet Zachary got a bullet in the back from that cowardly bastard."

Shrugging, Andy climbed back into her saddle. "Either way, dead is dead. Zachary is and Mister Jenks isn't. That's all that ever matters when you're playing for keeps."

Even Clint couldn't say much against that kind of logic.

"So what do we do about this ambush that's supposed to be waiting for us?" Con asked.

"If there is an ambush, then it's probably going to happen in that gorge over there. That's the only pass that would give Pearson any advantage anyway. Once we're through there, the rest of the way to Old Mexico is desert and flat-lands." Andy tugged on her reins until her horse was facing the rocky pass in the distance. "Besides, I know how Pearson thinks. They'll be waiting for us there if there's an ambush at all.

"That's a perfect test for Mister Jenks over there. If we meet up with Pearson, then we know he was telling the truth."

Fixing his eyes on Clint, Stamper asked, "And what if we don't see nothin' but prairie dogs and coyotes?"

"Then you can put a bullet into him," she said without even the slightest trace of emotion. "And you won't even have to ask permission."

ELEVEN

One of the biggest differences between the land east and west of the Mississippi was in judging distances by using nothing more than the naked eye. To someone traveling in the woodlands of the northeast or even in the fields down south, they could develop a knack for eyeballing how far a mile was or even how long it would take to ride to a certain point.

Once that same person crossed over into the wide-open prairies or deserts of the west, those eyeballs suddenly didn't seem so reliable. Mountains loomed in the distance and didn't get any closer after a full day's ride. It almost seemed like a trick developed for the pioneers to dangle a destination in front of them, only to keep moving it farther away as the oxen and mules struggled toward them.

It wasn't impossible to judge those distances, but it most certainly took a different set of eyes. And sometimes, even the most experienced traveler could be fooled. Especially in the desert.

When Clint had first caught a glimpse of the gorge farther along the trail, he'd thought it to be no more than half a day's ride off, at the most. Then, as he'd ridden alongside all the others in Kinman's gang, Clint was able to watch as the desert haze lifted from the scenery to reveal that the rocks seemed not to have gotten even the slightest bit closer.

They still sat far off where they could never be touched, tempting all the riders with promises of progress through a never-ending expanse of flat, sandy plains. At times, the clouds overhead seemed easier to reach then those damn rocks. Even Clint, who'd had his experiences with the tricks that could be played with natural landmarks setting out in too much open space, had allowed himself more than once to think that they were almost at the end of the road.

What made the waiting almost unbearable was that, if they rode through those rocks without so much as a shot fired at them, those rocks would indeed mark the end of his road. They rode through the day without more than a dozen words passing between them. The gang seemed almost reverent in their silence and reluctant to take their eyes away from the ever-looming rocks that spurred them on.

Finally, the daylight started to trickle away, leaving the sky a brilliant purplish color rather than the washed-out blue that had been overhead since morning. With the rich colors came a drop in temperature that hit them all like a cold fist in the stomach. Within minutes, the wind had transformed from an arid blast of heat to a cold, steely set of claws that tore through all the way down to the bone.

From the middle of the group, Andy raised her hand and let out a sharp whistle. "Everybody hold up," she said just loudly enough to be heard by all. "We're camping here tonight and leaving at first light, so everyone get your rest. Tomorrow, we'll be heading through that pass and then on into Old Mexico."

The convoy ground to a halt like a toy that hadn't had its key turned. Even though half of the outlaws barely even acknowledged that they'd heard Andy's words, every last one of them pulled their horses to one side and began going about the task of putting together a pair of campfires.

There was just enough scraps of wood lying about to build a small stool while only coming up two legs short. Even so, by the time the dark purples of the sky shifted into deep, velvety reds that led inevitably into black, there

were two pitiful fires sputtering on either side of the trail.
Men walked back and forth between them to get food and
trade bottles of whiskey in an attempt to fight back the
approaching bitter cold.

By this time, Stamper had lost some of his interest in
Clint, but not enough to let him get out of sight. The rifleman sat hunched over a plate of lukewarm beans and glared
at Clint over a flame that fought for its existence in the
middle of a small pit dug out of the sand. The only time
he looked away was when Andy came to sit down by
Clint's side, offering him a mug of steaming coffee.

"Mind if I join you?" she asked.

Clint turned to face her and pulled his coat a little tighter
around himself. "Do I mind? After a day in Mister Stamper's company, I wouldn't mind sharing a few moments
alone with a scorpion. At least those little buggers don't
stare at me for hours on end."

Laughing, Andy handed over her mug and positioned
herself so that she was directly between Stamper and Clint.
"You'll have to excuse him. He doesn't much care for new
faces."

The coffee was the liquid equivalent of someone lacing
twine through his eyelids and pulling them up over his
head. It was thick, oily tar that had been heated over the
opposite fire to syrupy perfection. In other words, it was
the best thing Clint had tasted in a long time.

"Who made this?" Clint asked after downing half of the
brew.

"I'm afraid that would be me," Andy said with a sheepish
grin. "Try not to drink too much at once or you're liable
to keel over."

The firelight danced across her features in a way that
made her skin seem to be a deeper shade of brown and her
hair to be even more vibrant and alive. Andy had unbut-
toned the top few hooks of her blouse, allowing the garment
to fall open just enough to reveal the smooth line of her
ample cleavage. She leaned forward slightly to toss the rest
of her own coffee into the fire, making sure to let her hair
drift casually over Clint's hands.

"Can I ask you a question, Andy?"

Letting out a deep breath, she held the still-warm mug between her hands and tilted her head slightly. "First, can you do me a favor?"

"What's that?"

"Call me Andrea."

Clint couldn't help but laugh at the frustrated look that had suddenly come across her face. "You've got to admit that you bring that on yourself. Why all the secrecy anyway? I mean, half the people in the area probably think your big partner over there is the true Andy Kinman," Clint said, pointing over toward Con.

"It's a man's world, Jenks," she answered. "In my line of work, you live or die by how much respect you can get. And when you can't get respect, you need to rely on fear. A woman just doesn't get much of either. That's God's honest truth."

Hearing her call him by his false name struck Clint as something of a shame. Andrea's voice was as smooth as the desert sky and silky as the sand. At that moment, he wanted to hear her call him by his true name, if only in part.

"I've got a confession to make," he said.

Andrea's expression darkened somewhat, but not enough to remove the seductive smile from her lips. "Let me guess . . . you shot Zachary in the back."

"No, nothing like that. My name is Clint."

She looked him over as though trying to see if he was hiding anything else. All the while, she didn't show him the first sign of disappointment or suspicion. Instead, she simply asked, "Is the last name still Jenks?"

"Yes," Clint lied. "But the first will do just fine. I hope that you don't—"

"Forget about it, Clint. After what Zachary tried to do to me, giving the wrong name doesn't seem so bad. I might even be convinced to let it go completely if you give me the proper incentive."

Without hesitating an instant, Clint leaned over and pressed his lips against Andrea's. They felt every bit as soft as they looked and tasted twice as sweet. When he tried to pull away after the first kiss, she reached up to slip her fingers through his hair and keep him from moving another inch.

Andrea's mouth opened to let Clint's tongue slip inside and gently trace along the edge of her own. She moved in closer until her body was pressed against his, and moaned slightly when Clint's hand began roaming along the side of her breast. Moving her fingers along the inside of his thigh, Andrea savored the feel of his muscled legs and the growing hardness between them.

Suddenly, Andrea pulled away. Although the space between them was less than an inch, it might as well have been a chasm for all the frustration it caused.

"Hold on," she said. "This isn't right."

"Feels right enough to me," Clint said as he moved in to get another taste of her moist, ripe lips.

"We can't do this." Looking quickly over her shoulder and then back again, Andrea fixed Clint with a pair of sultry eyes that danced with sparks of light captured from the nearby fire. "Stamper is still watching us."

The mere mention of the other man's name was enough to make the cold breeze send a sobering chill through Clint's body. "You want me to shoot him?"

Standing up, Andrea held a hand out to Clint and suppressed the laugh that tickled the back of her throat. "I think it would be easier if we just moved." Although her voice still had the same authoritative edge to it for the benefit of her men, the woman's intentions were a sultry current running beneath the tones.

It was that part of her that Clint obeyed as he got to his feet and followed her into a nearby patch of shadows.

TWELVE

The cold wind whipped over the desert sands, through the barren branches of several dead trees and over the backs of slumbering reptiles. Those same breezes traveled the distance between Kinman's camp and the distant pass through the rocks just so it could gain a voice as it howled between the narrow gorge.

On top of those rock formations, wearing several layers of battered denim and stitched cotton, was a solitary figure holding a rifle and spyglass in a small bag slung over his shoulder. That same figure scrambled up the side of the rocks like one of the native lizards winding its way through the sand. His fingers somehow found the next shelf built into the stone just as his toes slipped into a groove that was just big enough to be of any help.

Once at the top, the figure strode over the rock and sat down facing the campfires burning in the distance. The spyglass came out of its case and was pointed toward those fires, bringing him close enough to count the bodies gathered around the flames.

Bonnie Pearson glared through the lens and surveyed the rival gang. She knew when Zachary hadn't reported back to her that he'd either been killed, captured or convinced to go back to Kinman's side. Whichever it was didn't concern Bonnie too much since it all meant the same thing to her: Zachary was out of the picture.

Good, she figured. One less person to split the prize with.

If Zachary had been taken out after serving the purpose Bonnie had needed from him, that was all the better. She never did have much use for turncoats, anyway. Even if that turncoat was working for her at the moment, it would only be a matter of time before that person decided to switch sides again. After all, there was no going against the nature of a thing. That had been a lesson she'd learned too many times the hard way.

All she needed was for Kinman to ride in the direction of this gorge and try to move down south once she was on the other side. Bonnie had known Andrea too long to try a simple ambush while the gang rode through the pass. That would be too easy for Kinman to ready herself against.

No, all Zachary had needed to do was get Andrea fired up about moving to Old Mexico sooner rather than later. Once Andrea was in motion, Bonnie knew there would be no stopping her. Even if she knew there was a trap waiting for her, that woman would keep on riding out of sheer stubbornness.

Bonnie searched the distant campsite, slowly counting heads and taking mental note of how many of the gunmen actually seemed ready for a fight and how many thought they were simply spending a night under the stars. On the other side of the gorge, Bonnie's gang had already posted guards and put out their fires to make sure that they wouldn't be spotted. They knew damn well what they were fighting for and weren't about to take a chance on losing it.

Bonnie didn't believe in gambling. Instead, she believed in planning the best way to complete a job, follow through and then move on to the next one. With enough planning, there was no such thing as a gamble. Everything from military operations to bank robberies could run with clockwork precision if enough care was given to the details.

And details, as was blatantly obvious at the moment, was not Andrea Kinman's strongest suit.

Watching through the spyglass, Bonnie zeroed in on Andrea as though she was sighting through a rifle's scope. By the looks of it, Andrea was spending more than her fair amount of time with one of the newer members of her gang.

Either that, or she'd somehow picked up a stray along the way to Old Mexico. Leave it to someone like Andrea to conduct her business in such an unprofessional manner.

A set of footsteps crunched on the gritty sand behind Bonnie. Although the person approaching was trying to move as silently as possible, they knew better than to try and sneak up on her.

"That you, Nelson?" she asked.

The footsteps stopped less than ten feet away from her. "Yeah, Bonnie," came a smooth, quiet voice, "it's me. Just thought I'd check to see if you found anything interesting up here."

"Just where Kinman is camped out along with her gang. Looks like she'll be paying us a visit tomorrow."

"Hell, I could'a told you that much. You'd have to be deaf not to hear that many horses bearing down on your tail like that. They ride like a goddamn stampede."

"I prefer it that way. Makes it that much easier for me to keep track of where she is and where she's headed."

Nelson was a man who stood just under six feet tall and had the build of a man who'd forged through a lifetime of hard work. His skin was tough and calloused after spending years beneath the desert sun and his thick, rumpled hair was the same color of the sand covering the ground. A scraggly beard resembling a rat's nest built out of dirty straw sat upon his face, covering a tangled collection of ugly scars. One such scar ran all the way up his left cheek and ended right beneath his hairline. A dusty black patch covered what was left of that eye and was held in place by a chewed leather strap.

"Looks like that traitor did his job well enough," Nelson said.

Bonnie took the telescope away from her eye and got to her feet. She enjoyed looking down at creation spread out below her. Especially when she was fairly certain that the people in her sights didn't know they were being watched. "He's dead, you know."

Nelson stepped up to Bonnie's side and glared down at the distant campfires with his one good eye. "Who is? Zack?"

"Yes. Got killed in that saloon as soon as Andrea charged out of town. I heard some card player did the honors."

Spitting onto the ground and then rubbing it in with his boot, Nelson stared down at the ground as though he was grinding his toe into a spot of freshly spilled blood. "Probably for the better. That skunk would've just come back to us asking for more money. Either that, or he would've sold us out to Kinman or even the law, depending on who paid him the most."

"Funny," Bonnie said as she lifted the telescope to her eye once again. "No matter how valuable a traitor can be, he's still damaged goods." She stared down at her enemies for a few seconds before adding, "I'm still not even convinced tomorrow is such a good idea."

A look of shock jolted across Nelson's features, tugging awkwardly at the corners of his mouth. "But it was your idea to begin with and I still think it's a damn good one. Getting rid of Kinman and her men so early makes us look stronger and takes out a good chunk of our competition."

"I know, but if any of them survive, they'll be that much more fired up to beat us when all that money's on the line. This is the type of thing that needs to go off exactly as planned or not at all."

"Did you get a look at the card player that took out Zack?" Nelson asked.

Bonnie thought about the man she'd seen with Andrea no more than two minutes ago. "I wasn't there, but there's some new guy in Andrea's camp right now."

"Do you think he's the one?"

"There's no way for me to be sure."

"Then I say we should go ahead with the way we had things planned to begin with. Even if she knows we're here, she brought her men too damn close to avoid us. Whether they go through this pass or not, we can still ride in and face them down. It may get messy, but Kinman's boys ain't got no prayer against us. You know that for a fact."

"Do me a favor," Bonnie said as she stepped away from the edge of the rock. "See if you can recognize the new blood in Andrea's camp."

Nelson reached out and accepted the spyglass from Bonnie's hand. He knelt down so that his toe hung over the side of the rock formation and placed the scope to his eye. After taking a few moments to survey the others, he searched for Andrea Kinman. "I can't find her," he said after a while.

Bonnie crouched down beside him and pointed into the darkness. "She was heading off away from the fire on the right side last time I checked. It looked as though she was trying to get the other man alone or at least far enough away so that the others wouldn't hear what they were saying."

It took another minute or so, but Nelson eventually found what he was looking for and a crafty smile slid onto his face. "Ohhhh . . . I got her now." Andrea Kinman was easy enough to miss when she was dressed up to ride on the trail. The clothes she wore did a good job of concealing her figure. Even the way she walked made her blend in with a good amount of her men. Once he concentrated a bit on each figure individually, it wasn't so hard to pick out the other gang's leader.

"That man she's with," Nelson said while studying the pair from afar. "Is that the one you're talking about?"

"Yes. Have you seen him before?"

Nelson squinted through the glass for a bit longer. "Hard to say. He's doing a good job of keeping his back to us. Does he know he's being watched?"

"I don't see how he could."

The more Nelson studied the other man, the more uncomfortable he became. Although he couldn't make out much more than a shape and pattern of movement, there was something about that one that didn't sit right with Nelson. Maybe it was the way that other man acted as though he knew exactly what was going on and just how to position himself to keep his face hidden. Or maybe it was the simple fact that he was an unknown factor, which was exactly what Nelson hated more than anything else in the world.

"Come on, stranger," Nelson grumbled to himself. "Let's get a good look at ya."

The one-eyed man felt a jolt of nervous energy shock his system when the man he was watching looked up and turned around as though he'd heard Nelson's silent plea. He was still too far away and too dark to get a good look at the other man, but Nelson could see enough to know a few things.

"He ain't never been with Kinman before, I can tell you that much," he said. "And he's no stranger to being on the run, either."

Bonnie kept her eyes trained on the campsite even though, without the use of the telescope, it was nothing more than a collection of slowly shifting shadows around a set of glowing embers. "How can you tell all that just by watching him from back here?"

"Part of it's instinct," he said, still closely watching the way the new arrival circled Kinman and carefully scanned the rest of the camp. "Part of it's experience." Handing over the telescope, he waited until Bonnie was looking through it and then began running his fingers through the thick tangle of his beard.

"Look at the way he moves," Nelson pointed out. "He paces kinda the way a cat does when it's sneaking up on a field mouse. But at the same time, he's careful not to pace too much, so's he doesn't look suspicious."

Bonnie watched the stranger and listened to Nelson's words, putting them together to form a quick lesson in human behavior.

Wrapped up in his subject, Nelson went on. "He's looking over Kinman's men and keeping his eye on Andrea as well. When I saw him, he looked like he was counting how many were in the camp before turning his eyes this way and working out a whole other set of problems in that head of his."

"Do you think Andrea knows what he's doing?"

"Whether she knows or not, it doesn't matter. Besides, from what I saw, she was too interested in other things to concern herself much with what he was doing. But Andrea's not a stupid woman."

"No," Bonnie said, shaking her head. "She's anything but stupid."

"Exactly. So that means that she must already think she's got him figured out."

THIRTEEN

Although they'd only walked ten or twenty yards away from the fire, Clint felt like he'd suddenly stepped into the middle of nowhere. It didn't take long for them to be outside the fire's dimly illuminated circle and almost immediately the desert air began to chill his skin.

"I thought it was supposed to be hot in this part of the country," he said jokingly.

"Not at night," Andrea replied. "As soon as that sun goes down, it takes all the hot with it." Shrugging her shoulders, she slid off her jacket and let it fall to the ground. Beneath it, she was wearing a white cotton shirt that had obviously belonged to a man at one time. It was loose on her, but not enough to keep her supple curves hidden from view. "Well, maybe not all of the heat."

Clint took in the sight of her as he slowly stepped closer. The pale moonlight shone down on her to reveal the shape of her figure through the fabric of her clothing. Andrea's hands brushed over her body through the material, sliding over her hips and waist before tracing up to gently brush over her breasts. When she lowered her arms, her nipples were firm and standing erect beneath the constricting fibers of her shirt.

Clint walked up to her and put his hands on her hips.

54

She wriggled within his grasp and pressed up closer against his chest.

"Is this how you treat all your prisoners?" he asked.

"Only the ones that I want to make love to." She stated those words as simple fact while deftly unbuttoning Clint's shirt and slipping her fingers beneath the material. "Besides, just because I haven't quite made up my mind about you doesn't mean you're a prisoner."

Taking hold of her shirt and sliding it down over her shoulders, Clint looked at the way the moon's light played off of her deeply tanned skin. The tops of her breasts were exposed now, and Clint stopped there, wrapping the clothing tightly around her and pulling her in close. "If I'm not a prisoner, then you can give me back my gun."

Andrea's full lips turned up into a wicked grin and her eyes locked onto Clint's. "The only gun you'll be needing," she said as her hands slid over his stomach and down to the bulge in his crotch, "is this one."

Leaning down so that his lips brushed against the side of Andrea's neck, Clint kissed her skin and nibbled all the way down her shoulder. From there, he let the tip of his tongue touch gently onto her skin. She smelled like the desert breeze and had a taste about her that was an indescribable combination of sweet and salty. When he moved his lips up to her ear and began closing his teeth around her earlobe, Clint heard her start to breathe heavier. Her hands began working harder between his legs.

She was rubbing him with both hands through his jeans in slow, steady strokes that sent shivers beneath the surface of Clint's skin. Whenever Clint's tongue hit a spot that she particularly liked, she rewarded him by cupping his penis and squeezing just tight enough to make him moan beneath his breath.

"Do you always get this worked up before getting into a gunfight?" Clint asked as his eyes wandered away from Andrea and over to the formation of rocks farther along the trail.

Andrea's hands worked their way around until they were holding tightly onto his backside. Once she had a firm hold on him, she pulled him in closer and thrust her hips forward until she could feel his hardness rubbing against the warm spot between her legs. "If you think this is something, you should see me when the law's on my tail. You wouldn't be able to walk for days."

"You know they can probably see your fires, right?"

"Actually," Andrea whispered as her fingers traced around his waist and then down the front of her own body, "they're probably watching us right now. Pearson's got plenty of men with her, but she usually doesn't have much to do with them. I think she likes watching me." Shifting her hips back and forth while pulling down with her hands, she peeled off her pants and grabbed hold of Clint's hands so she could force them apart. Her shirt tore open easily, exposing beautiful round breasts that were even bigger than Clint had imagined. "Maybe we should give her something really good to watch for a change."

The chilled winds ran over her body, leaving her skin taut and quivering in its wake. She shivered slightly while looking at him with excited anticipation in her eyes. Her skin seemed to gain a kind of dull radiance when mixed with the moon's glow and her hard nipples cast small shadows along the curvaceous form of her breasts.

Clint could wait no longer. His eyes had been feeding on the sight of her ever since Andrea had sat across from him at the poker table back in Los Gatos. Since then, he'd been watching the way she moved and savoring the way she teased him with those rich brown eyes. Now that she had her hands on him, Clint's body had been screaming for him to get more of her.

He could smell nothing but her skin and could taste nothing but her flesh. He could see nothing but Andrea's naked body standing before him and no longer cared if it was the right time or the right place. All he knew was that he had to have her.

Soon, his skin was tingling with the cold touch of the desert, only to be heated up again by Andrea's wandering hands. She worked him out of his clothes until they were both standing naked in each other's arms.

Now, it was her lips tracing across his skin. Craning his head back to let the sensations wash over and through him, Clint looked up at the bright splash of stars that covered the heavens like a billion diamonds winking down at him, floating invitingly just out of his reach.

Andrea's lips felt warm and soft on the inside of his leg. She flicked her tongue out for just a second before nibbling playfully on his flesh. Her teeth sampled him here and there, biting just enough to give him a brief moment of pain before running her tongue over him to take it all away.

Threading his fingers through her hair, Clint looked down to see her face illuminated only by the trickle of light that bled down from the sky. Her eyes twinkled up at him and her lips glistened with moisture. Clint was about to say something when he felt the heat of her breath on the head of his penis and then the warm wetness as her mouth enveloped him. When he looked back up at the sky, Clint thought for a moment that he could leap up and fly toward those stars and pluck one down for himself.

Nelson dug a cigarette out of his shirt pocket and struck a match on the heel of his boot. He touched the flame to the end of the smoke and took in a few long drags. "You want to know what I think?" he asked.

Bonnie turned so that she was looking at him head on. "Always."

"I think you should always go with your first instinct. Those are usually the ones that come from your gut and your gut's got no reason to lie to you."

Shaking her head slowly, Bonnie thought about those words and considered them harder than if they'd come from any other member of her gang. She knew he was right. But there was always that part of her that loved to look for the flaws in every little thing.

"However this ambush winds up tomorrow, a lot of men won't even make it through the tournament. No matter who comes out on top, it'll be a bloodbath."

FOURTEEN

Kneeling before Clint in the cool darkness, Andrea moved her head back and forth, running her tongue along the length of his shaft while tightening her soft, juicy lips around him. She lingered at the tip for just a second, moving the end of her tongue in slow circles, teasing him before swallowing his entire length once again.

She slid his cock into her mouth again and again, each time sucking a little harder until he was about to explode. At the last second, she moved her head away and got to her feet, running her nails up over his skin as she did.

"You still think they're watching us now?" she asked.

Clint could barely form the words as he allowed himself to be pulled down by Andrea's insistent hands. "I'm lucky I can still remember who *they* are. Do you mean the ones that are out there . . . waiting for a chance to kill us?" he asked, recalling how she reacted to the thought of danger.

This time was no different. Andrea's body tensed against him as they sat huddled together in the sand. She reached up to run her fingers down along his chest and then behind his neck. From there, she pulled him closer so she could kiss him long and hard on the mouth. She nibbled on his upper lip as though she was starving for another taste of him and raked her fingernails across the back of his shoulders.

"They might be riding down here any minute," she said between gasping breaths.

They were sitting facing each other with legs entwined. Suddenly, Andrea placed both hands on Clint's chest and pushed him back with enough force to slam his back against the ground. Clint braced himself and landed with a dull *thump*.

One moment, the stars were once more spread out before him and the next, they were eclipsed by Andrea's body as she leaned down to continue their kiss right where it had left off. She positioned herself directly over Clint, straddling him with one leg clamped tightly on either side. As soon as their lips broke contact, she crawled forward until she was sitting on top of his chest.

Looking down at him, she arched her back and reached up to cup her breasts, squeezing them until her eyes clamped shut and her breath caught in the back of her throat. Andrea's nipples stood completely erect and Clint moved his hands up to cup her firm buttocks.

She took his unspoken demand and inched forward until her glistening pussy was less than an inch from his mouth. The soft, downy hair between her legs was damp with her moisture, only to grow even wetter when Clint buried his tongue in between her sensitive lips.

Reveling in the intense pleasure he was giving to her, Andrea ran her hands over her body and then reached back to stroke Clint's waiting cock. She loved the feel of it in her hands so much that she turned around so that she was sitting astride Clint's face while facing the lower part of his body.

The new angle brought Clint's tongue to new areas inside her, almost forcing her to cry out several times as his tongue probed between her legs. When the urge to scream became too much to bear, she dropped her body forward and took him in her mouth once again, this time sucking him in long, rhythmic strokes.

He took his time looking at her, soaking up every curve and every inch of flesh that was exposed to the moonlight.

It wasn't the first time Nelson had admired the way Bonnie's slender, supple form filled out her tight-fitting shirts or the easy curve of her hips, which led down to a pair of elegantly shaped legs. She somehow managed to keep her skin from turning into dried up leather, even after spending years in the harsh New Mexican territories.

Bonnie had the thick, wild red hair that many women would have killed for. It flowed around her face like a cascade of fragrant curls that were rarely let out of the restraining tail that hung down just past her shoulders. Her thin, bow-shaped lips were the same color as her hair; another feature that had filled Nelson's dreams more than once.

Although she did a good job of carrying herself with strength and authority, those qualities were not enough to dampen the feminine beauty that radiated from her like beams from the moon. In fact, her strength only enhanced her natural beauty, giving her an edge of danger to add spice to her overall package.

Nelson was no stranger to Bonnie's body. They'd shared a few moments over the years, but she simply wasn't the type to get her pleasure so simply. She needed to feel the excitement of lead flying through the air and the intrigue of living life in a constant struggle against mortal danger.

Bonnie was the kind who invited death, just so she could be the one to turn it away. She'd earned the respect of an entire gang of outlaws, which made her a truly dangerous woman. The gun at her side was there for more than show and Nelson had seen her prove that fact more than once.

Suddenly, Nelson was aware of how long he'd been staring at Bonnie. His eyes had locked onto hers and stayed there, longing for nothing more than another few minutes of her company. It was a dance that they'd been through too many times, however, and neither one of them really thought they had a chance of staying together for much longer than the length of an average heist.

"So now that we know about that stranger down there and that he's more than just some card player," Bonnie said, "what do you think we should do about him?"

"It's not my place to say," Nelson replied. "I'm not the leader of this gang."

"Give me your opinion, then."

"My opinion is that we're too close to a big score to worry about a wild card being tossed into the deck. It might even be that Kinman brought him in to fight on her side in the tournament."

Bonnie got a sour look on her face when she heard that part. "I was afraid you'd say something like that."

"Well, it's something to consider." Nelson took another look down at the enemy camp and tried to imagine that he could see not only the eyes of the men down below, but what was going on in their thoughts as well. It was a trick that brought about the occasional revelation, but wasn't doing much good for the moment. "I might like to go down there myself and take a look around."

"I don't want you to do that. We can't risk losing—"

"There ain't no risk, I'm tellin' ya. That bitch down there doesn't know how to run a half-assed search party, not to mention a gang that's worth its salt. I could be in and out of there before any of them bothered taking a look over their shoulder. All I need is to get within rifle range and I could pick off that stranger along with a few others in Kinman's little group, starting with that big son of a bitch that's always at her side."

"I've heard stories about Con being able to sniff out an attack in the middle of a rainstorm." Bonnie turned away from him and thought it over. Before too long, she wheeled around to face Nelson and shook her head rigidly. "I can't let you do it. Besides, we don't need to do much of anything besides get ready to tear through them at the first trace of sunlight tomorrow morning."

FIFTEEN

Andrea crawled forward along Clint's body, running her mouth down the length of his cock and then brushing her lips along the inside of his thighs. She closed her eyes and concentrated on how good it felt to have his tongue probing up inside of her. The effort it took to move her pussy away from his mouth was almost too much for her to muster. But she got herself to pull away from him and slide her body farther down.

Clint's body was on fire with the passions that had been ignited deep inside his flesh. Craving to taste more of her, he sat up and reached out for her, grabbing hold of one of her legs as she slowly crept toward his feet.

"Where do you think you're going?" he asked.

Tossing her hair back as she looked over her shoulder, Andrea straddled Clint's hips and lifted herself up into a squatting position. "I think I'm going to make you want to scream just as much as I do." And with that, she lowered her hips down to impale herself upon his rigid penis.

A powerful wave of fiery sensation swept through Clint's body like thousands of ghostly fingers tickling him from the inside. He lifted his hips up off the ground to bury his shaft deeper inside, their hips meeting halfway as Andrea leaned back to let her hair fall down to touch Clint's chest.

Clint reached around to massage Andrea's breasts, pinching the nipples occasionally to bring a quiet groan to her lips. They quickly found their rhythm as she bounced up and down while he thrust his hips toward her, burying his rigid pole as deep as it could go until Andrea's legs started to buckle beneath her.

"Don't stop," she pleaded in an urgent whisper. Unable to support herself where she was, Andrea straightened up and bounced on top of him a few times before leaning forward where she could brace herself with both arms. "Don't you ever stop."

From where he was, Clint couldn't help but admire the view. The perfect, sloping curve of Andrea's spine made a smooth line down her back. All of her hair had been swept to one side and the muscles in her back strained as she pumped her hips against his. Her backside was firm and tight, but not too much so that it lost its perfect, rounded shape. When she leaned forward a bit and craned her neck as the first waves of her orgasm began to rock through her body, the lips of her vagina tightened around his cock in a quick, erotic pulse.

Clint could feel the strength ebbing out of her, so he reached up to grab hold of her hips so he could thrust into her with renewed vigor.

"Oh my god, yes," she moaned, straining to keep her voice down low. "Do it to me harder. I want this to last all night."

Sweat was pouring off both of their bodies as Clint took control. He thrust up between her legs and held there, savoring the approaching climax that began rippling through his entire body. Andrea had gathered up her reserves of strength and had begun rocking back and forth. She reared up and clasped her hands to her breasts before running them down the sides of her body and reaching for Clint's legs for support.

SIXTEEN

A calm, comfortable silence descended upon the two figures sharing the top of the outcropping. It was the kind of silence that could only come about when everyone involved was intimately familiar with each other. Bonnie and Nelson looked out over the desert and thought about the fight that was scheduled for the following day.

It was going to be the first time the two gangs had met head-to-head since the feud between them had started. It had taken three years for those wounds to heal and now a fresh set of bloody swaths was about to be cut through the ranks of both rival factions.

Bonnie savored the oncoming violence the way a field general enjoyed the sensation of walking his chosen battlefield before the charge was sounded. Already, she could smell the gunpowder in the air and could hear the men shouting over the explosion of their weapons.

For Nelson, the evening was to be enjoyed for what it was, rather than what it preceded. He saw it as a sin to let such a cool, quiet night slip away without at least trying to soak up the comfort it provided. He would fight beside this woman just as he had for the last several years, but for the next few moments, he would close his eyes and relish the gentle caress of the stars upon his upturned face.

The peace lasted for a bit longer than normal: almost an entire five minutes this time.

"Only five more days until the tournament's over with," Bonnie said as she lifted the glass to her eye and stared down at the Kinman gang. "How many of them do you think we can pick off in that time?"

Nelson couldn't take his eyes off of the alluring redhead. It was moments like these, when she started talking like this, that he truly felt that he might be falling in love. "Five days? If they keep setting themselves up like they did here, I'd say we could take out the whole gang by tomorrow morning."

"You always were a little too optimistic."

"Never knew there was such a thing."

Peering through the glass, Bonnie scanned the entire camp and then turned around to look at the spot where her own men were sleeping. Compared to Kinman's settlement, the Pearson gang was nothing more than a collection of darker spots drifting among the shadows. There were no campfires lit and nobody walking about aimlessly. As a group, they made so little noise that if a person closed his eyes, he might just forget there was a gang there at all.

In fact, with the complete darkness that had settled over the desert, opening one's eye might not have helped much either. Only the occasional stray beam of moonlight shining down on a guard gave any hint of the gang's position. Bonnie nodded her head in grim satisfaction at the group she'd collected.

"I've been meaning to ask you something," Nelson said.

Still busy watching the way her guards had positioned themselves, Bonnie said, "Go on."

"None of the men would want to question you too much on what you're doing, but I know for a fact that they're all wanting to know exactly what it is they're getting into."

"That's understandable. I take it you've been listening in on what's going on down there. Picking up any bits of gossip and such."

Now, Nelson turned to look at Pearson's camp. In all, there were thirteen gunmen riding with him and Bonnie.

Handpicked from a wide assortment of killers and thieves, the gang had been blazing its way across the southwest for years without giving the law enough even to put a good picture together on what its leader looked like. Nelson had been there since the beginning and hadn't seen the likes of a fighting group like this since his years in the army.

The Pearson gang had so many kills under its belt that nobody even bothered counting anymore. So far, the only thing keeping them from wiping out Kinman's bunch was the other group's numbers and unpredictability. Kinman was always picking up extra gun hands and the fact that they acted like a bunch of wild dogs was a frustratingly effective way of countering Bonnie's structured tactics.

Acting as the gang's second in command, Nelson's job was to be among the rest of the gang whenever Bonnie couldn't. Since Bonnie had spent so much time dealing with getting them a spot in the upcoming tournament, Nelson had been working hard to keep the others together.

"I've been keepin' my ear to the ground," he said. "All anyone seems to know is that there's some kinda contest set up to see who can get their hands on a trunk full of gold and silver that's worth more than three hundred thousand." Nelson had to take a breath after mentioning that much money as something other than a fantasy. Even split among all of the gang, it would still make them all richer than they'd ever thought possible. "Actually," he said after it was obvious that Bonnie wasn't about to say anything, "that's about all I know of it, too."

Bonnie took the telescope away from her eye and set it onto the ground. After walking over to the edge of the rock facing Kinman's camp, she sat down and let her feet dangle over the side. The sandy gravel shifted beneath her weight, causing her to slide ever so slightly toward a nasty fall. The sensation of being so close to free fall was enough to send a chill through her system.

Looking up at the stars, which hung like silver lanterns in the sky, she allowed herself to smile widely and toss her hair back with a twitch of her neck. "If I tell you something, you've got to keep it to yourself."

Nelson's interest was piqued. "It wouldn't be the first time."

Looking like a little girl who'd been caught with her pockets stuffed with stolen candy, Bonnie looked down first and then back up at Nelson. "It's not three hundred thousand we're after."

"Oh really?"

"It's probably closer to six."

Already, Nelson could hear the men cursing at the top of their lungs and throwing out every threat imaginable. "Six thousand?" he asked, imagining what he would do when the entire gang turned against them for lying so badly.

"No . . . six *hundred* thousand. It's money that's been collected over the last five or six years. You heard of Tito Mondoza?"

"Yeah. He's the one hosting the tournament."

"Well, Mondoza's been into every kind of illegal business since he was old enough to pick up a gun. And ever since his first job back in lord knows when, he's been squirreling away part of his loot so he wouldn't have to be an outlaw forever."

Nelson gave a disbelieving laugh. "You mean he was fixin' to retire?"

"That's right. Only problem is that he got a little too good at his work." Bonnie paused for a second to let her own experiences wash through her mind. "After you kill for long enough, you need to keep killing just to keep ahead of those that make it their business to go after you. Steal for long enough and it gets hard to live any other way."

Listening to her, Nelson knew that she wasn't just talking about Mondoza. She was describing herself and him as well as the lives of everyone down in both of those camps.

"Mondoza knew he was in the life he'd chosen and couldn't get out," she continued. "But he still kept squirreling away that money. Habit, I guess. Well now he wants out and the only way he can do that is to make sure that nobody else out there has any reason to come after him anymore.

"He figures that getting rid of his money is the best way

to make all the thieves out there lose interest in him. Without all that cash laying around, he's nothing but some old Mexican with a dirty past."

"And what about the killers?" Nelson asked.

"They were the first ones Mondoza invited to his tournament. By putting up all that money as a prize, he knows that most of his enemies will wind up killing each other just to get at it. The rest will show up because it's one of the few times when so many can get so close to him. Knowing Mondoza, he'll be ready to pick off the ones he's worried about the most at any time during the tournament.

"Mondoza's got a healthy spread of land in a place called Rock Bottom, Arizona. From what I hear, everything in the town belongs to Mondoza. There's no law, and only a few others live there. Mostly it's just a ranch that got so big it applied for independence.

"Folks competing in the tournament fight their way to Rock Bottom and then shoot it out with the survivors once they get to Mondoza's place. The last one standing gets the prize."

Sure, it sounded simple enough. But after thinking about it for a few seconds, Nelson saw the brilliance in Mondoza's plan. It wouldn't take long before members of the same team would start killing each other and the more bodies that hit the dirt would be that many more steps for Mondoza toward a quiet retirement.

"He got ahold of me a few weeks ago and I convinced him to let my gang enter the contest. Told me that the prize was three hundred thousand in gold and silver, but I heard different. I heard that he's only putting up half of his money as an investment to get rid of anyone trying to get rid of him while the other half is set aside for that retirement fund he's been guarding for so long."

"Still squirreling it away, huh?"

Bonnie nodded. "You know what they say about old habits."

"Let's just hope they don't die as hard as Tito Mondoza."

A look of surprise came across Bonnie's face that didn't

even look convincing in the dim light provided by the desert moon. "Why, whatever do you mean?"

"I mean you were talking about getting our hands on six hundred thousand. You don't suppose he'll just give that to you because of that pretty red hair, do you?"

She ran her fingers through her hair and tilted her head in just such a way that drove any man crazy. Speaking in a soft, husky voice, she said, "If I try hard enough, I bet I could get a hell of a lot more out of the old bastard."

Nelson took a moment to catch his breath and hold back the desires that had reared up suddenly within him. "Actually, you just might. But something tells me that wasn't your plan."

Bonnie went from seductress to gang leader in less than half a second. One adjustment of her bearing brought out the woman that was much more familiar to anyone who knew her. "That old man's heart couldn't handle much of what I could give him. Besides, setting him up for the big fall shouldn't be too hard if we do it right and I'm sure it would be much more satisfying."

"That is, if we all make it through the tournament alive."

"Not all of us will make it out alive. Every one of my men should have enough common sense to know that much. But we've got enough of an edge and plenty of skill to see that enough of us survive to walk out with every penny that rotten son of a bitch ever stole during his entire miserable life." As she spoke, Bonnie's face grew more determined and her eyes became solidly fixed upon something that only she could see.

Her words took on a steely edge that was tempered by an underlying current of seething emotion that was very out of character for the calculating gang leader. When she'd spat out the last few syllables, she reached for a small pebble and pitched it into the darkness as though she was trying to get in the first strike against an invisible foe.

As much as Nelson wanted to press her about what could spark such emotion within her, he knew better than to do so just yet. There would be other times when he could make such an attempt. Any other time would be better than when she looked to be waiting for an excuse to spill someone's blood.

After a while, it looked as though the chilly air had cooled her down somewhat.

"We should start planning this out if we want to have a prayer against all the men that'll be coming to lay their hands on that money. Not to mention them that are there to get a piece of Mondoza himself. He's got enemies that I hate to even think about."

"There'll be plenty of time for that," Bonnie replied. "It's getting late and we both could use some sleep."

Nelson got to his feet and dusted himself off. He looked toward the other side of the pass and noticed that only one of Kinman's campfires were still burning. What was left of that one was only a faint glow resembling an afterimage floating in someone's vision after they'd accidentally looked at the sun.

"Looks like they've got the same idea," he said.

Reaching for the telescope, Bonnie flicked it open and lifted it to her eye. Once she'd found what she was looking for, she smiled widely. "Not quite. In fact, some of them look pretty damn busy."

Accepting the telescope as it was handed up to him, Nelson scanned the enemy camp and eventually caught a glimpse of Andrea and the stranger. Actually, he caught a glimpse of Andrea on top of the stranger.

"Oh my," he said. "They're not gonna get much sleep tonight."

"I'm surprised they can still move. I've been watching them do that for the last twenty minutes."

Nelson took another look through the spyglass. This time, he saw the stranger crawl out from beneath Andrea and move in behind her. "Now *that's* a good way to spend one of your last nights on this earth."

SEVENTEEN

All of the cold winds and chilled bones were nothing but a memory when Clint awoke the next morning. The low temperatures and silvery moonlight were washed away, to be replaced by an unforgiving sun that blazed down upon them all and lashed fiery tongues across their backs.

In the light of day, all of Kinman's men seemed to be no more than ten feet away from them at all times. Suddenly, Clint began to notice all the knowing glances thrown toward him and Andrea. Even the way they looked at him had gone from warning suspicion to reluctant acceptance.

As for the gang's leader, Andrea herself was nowhere to be found.

Clint busied himself by gathering up his belongings and helping himself to some of the food that was being prepared in one of the campfires, which had been resurrected from the night before. Breakfast consisted of beans and muddy coffee. If Clint wasn't so hungry, he wouldn't have even smelled the stuff if there was any way around it. When the food and drink combined in his mouth, it formed a noxious paste that nearly glued his mouth shut completely.

"How's the grub?" asked a man about Clint's age with short, cropped black hair and a dark red birthmark covering the better part of his face.

Clint tried to do his best to smile and nod approvingly.

When he tried to speak the first time, it was a chore just to get his gums apart. The second time was better, although his smile was worse for the wear. "It's not steak and biscuits, but I can't exactly complain."

"Ahhh, say what you mean," the man said as he chucked his plate to the ground and tossed the contents of his coffee mug behind him. "I've stepped in shit that tasted better than this."

"You've got a point," Clint replied with a smile. "But I've got a feeling that we won't be getting much better anytime soon."

The man grinned at Clint, watching him shovel in a few more spoonfuls of black, pasty beans. "Yeah, you worked up quite an appetite last night."

"You heard that, huh?"

"Hell, that woman probably woke up some of the coyotes in the next county." After wiping some of the spilled coffee from his hands, the man extended a calloused palm toward Clint. "Name's Jeffery."

Clint took the man's hand and shook it. "Clint Jenks."

"Hope you know how to use a gun, Jenks. From what I hear, you're gonna need it in a few hours."

Clint's eyes went automatically to the outcropping of rocks in the distance. "Actually, I've been meaning to ask someone about that. I don't suppose you've seen—"

"Seen what?" came a voice from off to the side of the fire. "This?"

As soon as Clint turned around, he saw something flying through the air toward him. Reflexively, he raised his hands to catch it, sending his plate to the sand. Even before he saw what it was that he'd caught, Clint recognized the weight and feel of the modified Colt in his hand.

Con stood towering over both men, looking rather amused at Clint's reaction. "Believe me," Con said while pointing to the pile of beans on the ground near Clint's feet, "you're better off tossing those than eating them."

Jeffery gave a short, snorting laugh. "If you ate that shit, you'd just toss it later anyway."

Clint tossed the spoon to the ground and flipped open

the cylinder of his pistol. It was empty. "This won't do me much good like this," he said.

Standing in the burgeoning heat of the early morning as though he'd been raised in the belly of a stove, Con looked down at Clint with an air of natural power. "If you need bullets for that thing, I'll get them to you. 'Til then, you can just keep hold of it and thank Andy for ordering me to let you have it."

Standing up, Clint placed the gun in its holster as though he was barely used to holding it. By the look on Con's face, the big man had recognized that pistol as a piece of deadly art.

Clint ignored the suspicion in the other man's eyes and turned to face the distant rocks. "I guess we'll be heading that way soon."

"Yeah," Con said with obvious distaste for the idea. "That's what she wants to do."

"It's not what you want to do, though, is it?" Clint asked.

Con looked like he was about to say something, but then thought better of it and kept his mouth shut. "You ain't been around long enough to start askin' questions like that, boy."

"It's all right," Clint said. "I think I just got my answer."

The look that Con gave him was enough to double the heat pouring down from the sky. For a moment, Clint thought he might actually need those bullets, but then Con turned and walked away.

Jeffery gave a low whistle from where he still sat by the smoldering fire. "You're either real stupid, or too damn brave for your own good. Since you ain't been around long enough to know Con like the rest of us, I'll be putting my money on stupid."

Clint looked around the camp and quickly spotted Andrea standing at the edge, facing the rock formation. He wound his way between the bustling gang members and walked up to her side.

"Are you going to tell me yet why exactly we're heading straight into something that looks pretty much like a trap?" he asked.

"Con was right the other day," she said by way of a reply. "You talk too damn much."

"Since I'm along for the ride now, could you at least tell me where we're going?"

Andrea had lost all the passion that she'd shown to him the previous night. Now, she moved and spoke as though all of that emotion had been pushed deep down inside where it wouldn't be in the way. She turned and started to walk away, but then she wheeled back around to look him straight in the eyes. Once again, Clint could see the emotion that was at the core of her being. Apparently, she couldn't push it down too far.

"There's too much at stake, Jenks," she said. "If we don't face them down now, then we'll just have to do it once we all get to Arizona."

Nodding, Clint said, "That's true enough, but at the tournament, won't the odds at least be even?"

Andrea shook her head and smiled grimly. It was the expression of someone trying to put their best face forward when staring into the eyes of their executioner. "If we let Pearson get to the tournament with her entire gang, I can guarantee you that we will not only lose, but that we'll all be killed the first day."

"I don't understand," Clint said, putting on a confused look that was so convincing mainly because it was damn close to what he actually felt.

Andrea told him all about Tito Mondoza and why he'd set up his tournament. She also told him about the old crime boss's motives for getting so many killers together in one spot.

"That's an awful dangerous way to get rid of your enemies," Clint said once she'd finished her explanation.

"Well, without so much money at stake, there wouldn't be half as many takers. The only problem is that Mondoza is more interested in cleaning up his affairs than running a fair competition."

Clint had heard about Mondoza, but only as a rumor circulated among outlaws who pointed to the man as something of a hero or twisted role model. "Then you're afraid

Mondoza will cut a deal with Pearson's gang to get rid of you?"

"As far as I know, most of the people in the tournament will be coming alone or maybe in pairs. Pearson's got one of the biggest groups coming to this thing. The smart thing to do would be to get her to take me out as soon as possible since she already knows me and has crossed my path more than a few times."

"But she couldn't kill you before, so—"

"She thinks like she's in the army or something. Usually, she takes credit for half the things my men have done anyway, so she figures that allowing me to live just makes her look better. Besides, we came to an agreement a while back and drew a line in the sand that we both respect. Well," Andrea said as a familiar mischievous smirk crossed her face, "I *usually* respect it. We have our dust-ups every now and again, but nothing close to the war it could be. And war is exactly what Mondoza thinks could take me as well as all of my men out of the picture."

Clint nodded, soaking all of this in while fitting the pieces together in his mind. There were a lot of things that bothered him, but one more than the others nagged at him the most. "Why is Mondoza going after you so hard? Do you have some history with him?"

"You could call it that," she replied. "He's my father."

EIGHTEEN

Clint had gone along with the Kinman gang expecting a lot of things. This hadn't been one of them.

He blinked his eyes several times and did a damn good job of looking surprised. "Tito Mondoza is your father?"

Wrapping her arms around her body, Andrea lowered her head and held herself as though the desert had suddenly gone cold. "I'm not exactly the pride of the litter, but yes. The only thing we have in common besides the side of the law we stand on is that neither one of us can remember my mother."

"I don't suppose you'd want to tell me why your own father would want to see you dead so badly?"

When he'd asked the question, Clint had mainly just been getting it out of his system. In no way did he expect to get much else by way of an answer besides maybe a slap in the face or a dirty look. Instead, Andrea took a deep breath and dropped her hands to her sides before looking up into his eyes.

"There's not a lot to it, really," she said quietly. "As soon as I got old enough to care about what my father did for a living, he started showing me every nasty little part of his business. I saw more men get killed by the time I turned ten than most soldiers see in a lifetime. He told me who the corrupt politicians were and how to get a lawman to sell his soul for the lowest price.

"When I was a kid, I thought it was actually kind of fun. I didn't get my hands dirty for quite a while, so all I got to see was how everyone treated me when they knew who I was. All I had to do was drop my father's name and I could walk out of any store with my arms full of whatever I wanted."

She'd been stepping closer to him as she spoke, but then broke away and looked to the ground almost as though her head had become too heavy to hold up any longer. "He gave me my first gun when I turned sixteen. He brought in a man and had some of the others hold him down. I was told to shoot that man or get out of his house forever."

Clint wanted nothing more than to believe the best about Andrea. But by the way she was holding herself and the way she refused to look him in the eye, he got the distinct feeling that her story didn't have a happy ending. "What did you do?" he asked.

"I turned the gun on my father and told him to give me enough money to make a start for myself in the world."

Clint's jaw dropped a little and his eyes widened. "You robbed Tito Mondoza? How much did you get off of him?"

"Fifty dollars. Even with a gun pointed at him, the old bastard refused to part with his precious money."

From what he'd heard about Mondoza, Clint could pretty much guess the rest of the story. But he listened anyway to see if there were any more surprises.

"When I first left, I heard there was a bounty out for me," Andrea said in a sad, faraway voice. "Two hundred dollars to tell him where I was. Five hundred to bring me back to him. I was so scared, I thought he wanted me dead. So I used every trick I'd learned and even made up a few of my own to avoid getting caught. There were enough of Father's contacts I could use once or twice to get together with some pretty rough groups."

A shadow passed over her face just then. Her voice trailed off and she wrapped her arms tightly around herself once again like she was mother and child all bundled up into one person. "I made it . . . barely. And I learned that men would do a lot of things for a woman, so long as they got what they wanted. Funny, but they always wanted the same thing." Andrea's hand drifted to her pistol and then the smile returned to her face. "Once I finally learned how to use one of these, that all changed. I took charge of my life as well as my men. After a few years, Father stopped trying to get me to come home and I woke up one day to find myself at the head of my own gang.

"In answer to your question, Mister Jenks, I am living proof that the great and powerful Tito Mondoza is not invincible. The way he sees it, I robbed him of his daughter, his old life, as well as his pride and of course fifty dollars. Nobody ever steals from Tito Mondoza. *Nobody*."

She spoke those last words the way a preacher might quote the Bible, punctuating them by gritting her teeth and fixing her gaze to that same outcropping of rocks as before.

"Sounds to me like this could all be settled by visiting your father personally," Clint said. "Maybe talking to him would go a long way to ending this thing between you."

Andrea shook her head. "It's been too long. We're way past that now. Besides, the old man is fixing to either die or disappear and he won't be in the mood to do much of anything besides making sure his road is as smooth as possible." Suddenly, the cloud lifted from Andrea's face and she turned back toward her camp.

The men were all but finished with their packing and the way she looked at them spoke volumes for how highly she regarded them as a whole. Con had been lashing some packs to the back of one of the horses and when he saw that Andrea was ready to acknowledge them again, he strode up to her side.

"We're all set to go," he said. "Just say the word and we'll be rolling out of here. Near as I can figure, we should make it to those rocks in less than half a day. Even quicker if we don't stop too often."

Clint turned his attention to the rocks. From what he could see, they were high enough to give plenty of advantage to anyone on top of them or waiting on the other side of the pass. "That whole place is a trap waiting to happen, but nobody seems too concerned about that," Clint said. "I still don't see what any of you expect to accomplish by riding straight into it."

"That trap is what Pearson is putting all of her faith into," Andrea replied. "Riding around it would waste time and lives since they would just be able to swoop down on us as soon as we got close enough or just pick us off with rifles from up top. So that doesn't leave us much choice."

Clint could feel the aggravation building up inside of him. He felt like the only sane man in a caravan of lunatics that were charging straight for the edge of a cliff. No matter how loudly he tried to warn them, they would just shrug and run toward their deaths that much faster. "The way I see it, we've got a real big choice that nobody seems to care that much about."

Con glared at him as though he was one second away from burying that machete of his deep into Clint's chest. When he started to surge forward with both hands balled up into ham-sized fists, Andrea stopped him with nothing more than an outstretched arm.

"No need, Con," she said. "Let him say his piece."

"Why don't we just head around those rocks and give them a wide enough berth so that even rifle fire couldn't hit us," Clint suggested. "We'd make better time and avoid an unnecessary fight before the tournament."

The look on Andrea's face was pure patience. She nodded before the silence got too uncomfortable and then asked, "Was that all?"

"Well . . . yes."

"Great." Turning to Con, she said, "Tell everyone to mount up. We're heading for those rocks as soon as possible."

Clint let out an exasperated sigh. "This would almost be funny if it didn't mean that I'd be dead by the end of the day."

Once she was in her saddle, Andrea looked down at Clint and winked. "There's one thing about all of this that I know and you don't, Jenks."

"What's that?"

"My father. He won't want his daughter damaged out here. Not like this. If Pearson's working for him like I think she is, then we're supposed to make it to Arizona alive and kicking."

"And what if you're wrong about Pearson?" Clint asked. "Why take that chance when we can just ride around this whole damn problem?"

"Because that wouldn't be any fun, lover." And with that, she touched her spurs to the sides of her horse, sending the animal into the desert at a full gallop.

More than a dozen horses thundered past Clint as he walked back to where Eclipse was waiting. The campsite was in the middle of a swirling cloud of dust and wild animals, giving Clint more than enough cover to slip away from the pack and head back to Los Gatos for a decent meal and another few days of poker.

To hell with the damn gangs, he figured. If they were so intent on killing each other, who was he to argue with them?

Clint was just about to give into this line of reasoning when he saw that not all of the horses had charged toward the awaiting battle. Con sat upon his horse looking big enough to break the poor animal's back.

"You've heard way too much to just ride away from us," the big man said. "Like it or not, you're in this until the end." He slid his machete halfway out of its scabbard and reflected the sun off its polished blade and into Clint's eyes. "But don't worry," he said while plucking at the edge of the blade with his thumb. "The end for you might come a lot quicker than you think."

NINETEEN

The rocky pass loomed ahead of them, growing larger with every step the horses took. Clint had allowed Eclipse to fall behind most of the group so he could get the opportunity to watch the others. Mainly, he was looking for how they would react as they got closer to what was surely an ambush.

Many of the gang looked resigned to the approaching fight, while others simply kept their faces turned down so they didn't have to confront what was coming. Every time Clint tried to talk to one of them, all he got in return was a suspicious glare or some halfhearted threat for disturbing their peace.

As for the smaller group riding at the front of the pack, there wasn't much that Clint wanted to hear from them that he hadn't already heard. He knew what Andrea would say to any questions because he'd already asked them straight to her face. He had a pretty good idea that Con would be waiting for some excuse to bat Clint away like a fly. And as for the rifleman they'd called Stamper, it was plain that he wasn't talking to much of anybody.

More than once, Clint thought about breaking character, if only to give the gang something else to think about. Anything just to turn them away from that everapproaching stand of rocks. There was something about that place that Clint just didn't like. The feeling wasn't based on anything he'd heard about either gang, or even on a particular fear of walking into a storm of lead.

The feeling was just that; a strange twist of his feelings that told him he was making a big mistake.

Perhaps it would have been better to break off from the group and let them shoot each other as much as they wanted. Perhaps the smart thing to do was to simply let them go about their business since many of them wouldn't be alive long enough to bother anybody else anyway.

There was no perhaps about it.

All of those things *would* have been the smart decisions to make.

But there was something else that kept him from turning Eclipse in a safer direction and moving on. It was an even worse feeling in the pit of his stomach that anything connected so directly to Tito Mondoza could be nothing but bad for anyone involved.

Mondoza had his fingers in a lot of pies and not one of them was sweet. Clint knew that if he let these gangs get to their tournament and fight their fight, he would hear about it later when the victors decided to make their presence known. For all he knew, the gang that won this tournament might just be the next Wild Bunch or some kind of similar terror to smear its bloody hands across the country.

Like it or not, Clint knew that Con was right. He was in this thing.

Right until the end.

Once it seemed like they were making progress in their ride toward the rocks, the formation seemed to swoop down upon them like a giant predator. They'd only just left the noon hour behind when the sand beneath the horses' hooves started turning into gravel. From there, the desert floor became hard and then the animals' steps were echoing off the nearby walls.

Clint flicked his reins and moved up to the front of the group. Although Con wouldn't allow him to get next to

Andrea, Clint still managed to get close enough to speak to her without yelling.

"Now what?" he asked. "Do you have any kind of plan or should we just keep riding until we start getting shot out of our saddles?"

Andrea's face didn't change as she looked around to scan the upper reaches of the pass. Suddenly, she pulled back on her reins and brought her mount to a stop. Without saying a word, she raised her left hand and made a fist.

Just then, Clint could hear all the others coming to a stop behind him. By the time he turned to look at where the rest of the gang had positioned itself, more than half of the others were turning around and heading as fast as they could out of the pass. Once there, they split up and headed along opposite sides of the formation.

"Pearson!" Andrea shouted once she figured her men had been given enough time. "You never were no good at sneaking up on me, so why don't you come on out. Maybe we can work this out without a scuffle."

For a moment, Clint thought that he heard the beginnings of a rockslide. Countless pebbles scratched against the edge of the pass as they fell from the top of the formation, which loomed at least thirty feet over their heads. The rocks looked like dead insects whose wings had been plucked in mid-flight as they tumbled down the side of the rocks and started raining down on the heads of those who'd ridden in below.

Clint tugged the brim of his hat down to deflect some of the rocks as they started pelting him from above. Following that sound was another kind of rumbling. This time, it was the thunder of horses hooves clomping against the bounders as riders moved in on them from all sides.

Just as suddenly as it had started, the rumbling came to a stop. The instant Clint looked up, he saw exactly what he'd been expecting ever since he'd heard that this pass even existed. He turned to his right and saw Con sitting in his saddle as though he was just admiring a scenic view.

"All right," Clint whispered to the big man. "How about handing over those bullets?"

Before Con could reply, a shot rang out within the confines of the rocks. The blast echoed within the cramped spaces and rebounded from all the jagged angles. Smoke wafted in the air and stung Clint's nose, drawing his attention to the source of the shot.

"Andrea?" Clint said in disbelief. "What the hell are you doing?"

"I'm getting this thing started," she said.

And no sooner had the words come from her mouth than the entire pass burst like a powder keg that had been struck by a cannonball. First came the sickening thud of a body hitting the desert floor after falling all the way from the top of the pass. Then, just as Clint had hunkered down over Eclipse and directed the stallion toward what little cover there was in the middle of the shooting gallery, the storm of lead began whipping back and forth, chewing at the air like a metallic swarm.

Some of the gunfire came from the upper reaches of the rocks where, Clint guessed, the rest of Andrea's gang had engaged some of the rival members. But most of the fire was being concentrated in the middle of the gorge where the leaders were scattering for their dear lives.

Instinctively, Clint snapped his Colt from its holster. Even as his brain was reminding him that there were no bullets in the chamber, his body was still getting ready to take aim and defend himself. Even though he knew he'd be riding into trouble, Clint most certainly did not expect Andrea to sign over their lives without more thought than she would give to stepping on a wayward ant.

Clint looked over to Eclipse, making sure that the Darley Arabian wasn't in any immediate danger. Although the stallion wasn't protected by much in the way of cover, none of the shooters seemed interested in anything that wasn't human. Although that wasn't exactly great news for Clint, seeing the horse did give him a ray of hope. Or, more importantly, the horse's saddle was what caught his eye.

Reaching up to flip over a blanket covering Eclipse's saddlebags, Clint saw that his prayers had been answered when he found his rifle right where he'd left it, strapped to the stallion's back. He launched himself forward just long enough to grab the rifle by the stock and pull it free of its holder. He worked the lever and felt hope surge through him at the sound of the familiar mechanism's well-oiled *click-snap*.

Those hopes sunk right down to his boots, however, when he realized that the rifle's chamber was empty as well.

An explosion of sparks burst within inches of Clint's face, causing him to pull back behind a rock, and hope that he was out of the line of fire. As soon as his back hit the boulder with nearly enough force to push the air from his lungs, Clint heard the sound of approaching footsteps hurrying in his direction. Putting on his best poker face, he held his rifle as though it was something more than decoration and prepared to greet his oncoming visitor.

At first, Con looked like he was about to put a bullet into Clint's skull out of sheer reflex. Then, once he put that impulse in check, the big man hunched over and threw himself next to Clint.

"Helluva way to start the afternoon, huh?" Con grunted.

Clint nodded and scrunched down lower as another hail of bullets sparked off the rocks above his head. "You got that right. I only hope we live long enough to see that tournament."

"What are you talkin' about? This *is* the damn tournament!"

TWENTY

Bonnie Pearson had been awake since before the crack of dawn, anxiously awaiting this very moment. She'd been unwilling to speak to any of her men or even eat more than enough breakfast that was required to keep her from falling over. It was all she could do to keep from running in nervous circles as she watched Kinman's gang approach slowly from the north.

Now that the air was exploding with fire and the wind stank of gun smoke, she felt truly alive. Nelson stood next to her on top of the rock formation, glaring down at the gunfight that had just blossomed into life. Men scurried about around and below them, settling into the positions that Bonnie had arranged the minute they'd pulled into the rocks more than a day ago.

It was perfect. As always, her men were moving just as she'd told them and firing in the order that would allow them to cover those that needed to reload. Watching Kinman's gang running about like decapitated chickens almost made the fight seem like a slaughter in the making.

Nelson was laying next to her, flat on his stomach and looking over the barrel of his Winchester rifle. "She played it just like you said she would," he said after sending a round into the top of a rival gang member's head. "Just rode right in and started shooting."

Bonnie had a rifle at the ready, but still hadn't fired it. She preferred to wait until she could get close enough to pull her pistols, holding back on the rifle until she saw someone in need of cover fire. "She's not exactly a hard person to read," Bonnie replied. "Every time we lock horns, this is how she's gone about it."

"Nearly beaten us more than once, too."

"Yeah, but not this time." Bonnie could hold out no longer. Handing the rifle over to Nelson, she got into a low crouch and pulled her Smith & Wesson. "Trade me for your side arm," she said, holding out her hand.

Nelson grabbed her rifle and plucked the .44 from his holster. Grudgingly, he gave her the pistol. "You know better than this, Bonnie. At least wait until we clear some of them others out of there."

"It's never a good time to run into a gunfight," she said while snapping back the hammer of one of the pistols and shoving the other into her holster. "Just get ready to back me up if I need it."

Before Nelson could say another word, she was scurrying toward a steep, narrow path that led down the side of the rocks. Already, he could hear more gunfire coming from that direction, but was unable to get a look to see which side was doing the shooting. Taking a deep breath, he shoved a few more cartridges into the breech of his rifle and slung Bonnie's weapon under his arm. Nelson then climbed to his feet and charged toward the front line.

Andrea stood in the middle of the pass for as long as she could. All around her, the ground was being chewed up by flying chunks of lead and the air was burning with acrid smoke. A wide grin formed on her face that only got wider as the firefight churned with full force.

She didn't need to look around to know that at least some of her men were trying to follow behind her. Knowing that Con had split off to go in his own direction, Andrea charged toward the enemy gang and squeezed her trigger with a primal scream.

A pair of Pearson's men emerged from behind a large

rock about ten feet ahead of her. As soon as she saw them, their faces disappeared in a cloud of chalky gray smoke. Andrea ducked her head and grit her teeth as the bullet whipped overhead and spun through the air behind her. Extending her arm and taking half a second to aim, she squeezed her trigger, putting a round through the other man's chest.

Something in the back of her mind told Andrea that she was running in the wrong direction. Before she could say anything to the men following her, she stepped to the side and heard another round sing through the air to smack solidly against flesh. Andrea dove for the cover of a nearby rock and turned to look at who'd been hit. All she could see were feet flying up in the air and a bloody mist smearing the space that had once been occupied by one of her followers.

Every part of her mind and body told her to get the hell out of that pass if she wanted to live to see another day. Her heart and soul, on the other hand, cried out for something drastically different. Those parts wanted to feel the heat of battle until it consumed her in its flame. The smell of spent gunpowder bit into her sinuses, and her heart was beating as though it was trying to kick its way out of her chest, but still she was compelled to go on.

It was either that or surrender. And that was no choice at all.

"Form up behind me," she shouted to any of her men who were close enough to hear. "We've already got men working their way to the top, so all we have to do is charge down the center and take down as many of them as we can."

There were three others within the sound of her voice and they were all more scared than they'd ever been in their entire lives. The three men had been with Kinman on some rough jobs, but never in all-out battle like this. They looked at one another for a hint as to what they should do next.

"I say we let her kill her own damn self," the first man said in a harsh whisper. "We can make our way back out or even join up with Pearson."

The second nodded while scanning the upper reaches of the pass. Although there were obviously some of his companions up there, it was impossible to tell which way the fight was going. "All I know is that if we stay here, we're dead men. I thought we were heading into a fight . . . not some goddamn war."

While the first two went about their hasty discussion, the third man crept forward to get a look at what Andrea was doing. What he saw made him stop and point at her in disbelief. "Look," he said.

The first man had been about to turn tail and run back the way he'd come when he heard that single command. Following it, he turned back to face the gang's leader. "I'll be damned."

She was still shouting orders and taking shots from the cover she'd found. Rather than turn around to look at her men, she spent those seconds aiming and picking rival gunmen off the side of the rocks. One at a time, three of Pearson's men jerked in pain and fell through the air, landing with a sickening thud onto the hard, stony ground. There was fire coming in from another spot inside the pass as well to aid in her efforts, but somehow Andrea was seeing that a way was being cleared for herself and her men.

Suddenly, it seemed to the trio that Mondoza's prize wasn't so far out of reach after all. In fact, it was looking as though charging forward was actually going to be easier than running away.

The second man steeled himself and then grunted. "What the hell. I could use a share of three hundred thousand dollars more'n a hole in the head." And with a battle cry rivaling Andrea's own, he bolted from cover to get to his leader's side.

The other two didn't have time to think. They were too busy exploding from the rocks and firing up into the approaching enemy as a fresh wave of bullets showered down upon them.

TWENTY-ONE

All around Clint there were sparks flying through the air, bullets whipping by and bodies running one way or another in the chaotic confusion of the spontaneous war created by the two rival gangs. Once he had a chance to get his wits about him, he realized that the situation wasn't quite as bad as it seemed mainly because there were less than two dozen actual participants to worry about. And even though the lead had been flying for only a few minutes or so, that number was going down with each passing second.

Clint pressed himself against the rock that was serving as his shield and looked over to Con, who seemed to be having the time of his life returning fire or covering the advance of more than ten of his fellow gang members.

"This is crazy!" Clint shouted over the constant roar of gunfire that had seeped into the pass like a fog.

Con took another shot, looked over to Clint and nodded enthusiastically. "Hell, boy, nobody's just gonna give away that kind of prize money. Here," he said extending his hand, "why don't you make yerself more useful?"

Looking over to what the big man was doing, Clint caught the sight of something moving directly behind Con's hulking form. At first, it was just a blur of motion that blended in perfectly with all the other chaos that had descended upon them, but then it took on a shape of its own and started rushing in closer to the rock that they were both hiding behind.

In the next second, that moving shape formed into a man that had dropped down to the desert floor and had begun rushing around Eclipse to charge straight for them both, with a gun in each one of its fists. One second it looked as though it might keep running, but in the next it focused in on Con and came in for the kill.

Clint acted out of instinct when he realized that he didn't have enough time to both act and think before Con was killed on the spot. First he lunged forward, coiling his legs beneath him like a spring so he could push off toward the big man. Then, dropping his rifle to the ground as he moved, Clint pushed toward Con while reaching for the holster at the big man's side as he moved by. Finally, he snatched the weapon that had been hanging to Con's right, and snapped his wrist forward as his momentum carried him along to meet the oncoming gunman at a point less than three feet away from where Con was standing.

Clint's eyes were trained on the gun coming toward not only Con but himself as well. It was that gun he saw as his wrist completed its whiplike motion that brought Con's machete up and out until the blade sunk solidly into the other man's stomach.

For a split second, Clint wasn't sure if the blade had struck home at all. Then, his arm seemed to get tangled up in the attacker's body while the rest of him slammed violently into the other man's shoulder. Suddenly, he found himself face to face with the snarling visage of one of Pearson's hired guns. Something heavy dropped onto Clint's toe before bouncing off onto the stony ground as something warm and wet began to surge over his clenched fist.

Clint stared into the gunman's eyes, trying to move his hand so he could do something before he or Con were blown off their feet. Then he noticed the gunman's face turn pale and blank. Looking down for an instant, Clint noticed that the thing that had hit his foot was the other man's gun. The warm wetness on his hand was that same man's blood.

Just then, Clint felt his entire body get pulled down by the weight that had suddenly been added to his side. He tried to move away, but was unable to get any distance between himself and the slumping figure that had fallen onto him like a sackful wet mud.

With one quick motion, Clint jerked the machete free from the gunman's body and let the guy fall. Since it was the only thing available to him that would do any good, the machete remained in Clint's grasp as he turned to look and see if there were any more coming in behind the first gunman.

Actually, there were two more coming around the rock with their pistols drawn and ready to fire.

Clint didn't let a second tick by before he raised the machete over his head and let out an almost feral cry. He could feel the other man's blood dripping onto his face as he took a step toward the remaining pair of shooters. For a heart-stopping moment, he thought that he'd just stepped into the final moment of his life screaming like a bloodthirsty savage. Then, the pair's faces dropped and all the color washed out of their skin as they chucked their pistols to the ground at Clint's feet and bolted in the opposite direction.

Con was still looking at Clint with his hand outstretched, an expression of equal parts awe and disbelief etched into his face. "Now that," he said, "is one of the damnedest things I've ever had the pleasure to see."

Although things had died down somewhat, the shots still echoed in the pass, causing Clint to pull himself back down behind the rock. The first thing he saw when he looked down to the hand Con was offering was the glint of sunlight off of several bits of metal. In fact, those bits were actually the six shells that had been confiscated from his modified Colt. At that particular moment, those bullets were the best things Clint could imagine seeing.

After exchanging the machete for his ammunition, Clint quickly loaded his Colt and scanned the sides of the rock. His eyes locked immediately onto a figure laying on his belly on a small ledge overlooking the pass. Clint recognized that man as the one that had been keeping him and Con pinned behind the rock for the last several minutes.

"Where the hell do you think you're going now?" Con asked as Clint snapped back the Colt's hammer and made his way around the rock.

The instant Clint broke from cover, he dove quickly to the side, narrowly escaping the first two shots that came his way. He then took a few steps forward, which put him in the middle of the road leading through the rocks and out of the line of fire from the shooter overhead.

Clint stood there for a second, waiting as long as he dared while being so completely exposed. He took a few quick steps, making sure that his boots made plenty of noise as they scratched along the rocky surface of the ground. There were isolated fights taking place above and on either side of him, but Clint kept his eyes focused on the wall of the pass, waiting for his chance.

Finally, the gunman that had been keeping him and Con pinned in place stuck his head out and swung his rifle around to put Clint down for good. The instant Clint saw the man, his Colt was in motion. Letting instinct and pure skill take over, Clint didn't even need to sight down the barrel. All he did was bring up the pistol as if it was an extension of his own hand. After that, the only thing left to do was point . . . and squeeze.

The Colt bucked once in Clint's grasp and sent a single round through the air and into the forehead of the man behind the rifle. His face snapped out of view, leaving behind a fine red mist that stained the air just as the man's brains now stained the rocks.

Clint waited for a second, straining his ears for confirmation that the other man wasn't getting up. When he heard the body thud and then slide down, he motioned for Con to follow him as he began running for the other side of the pass.

TWENTY-TWO

As he began making his way down the narrow path, Clint felt as though the rest of the world had been holding its breath for him to take that last shot and now it was rolling right along in all its sound and fury. Bullets cut through the air while men chased one another down. There was even the occasional body falling from the top of the rocks all the way down to the ground, but Clint kept his eyes trained on the path ahead, only firing the occasional shot when he could see a potential threat coming toward him.

It was only a matter of seconds before there was another set of footsteps moving along beside him. Con charged next to Clint, taking out one of Pearson's shooters before he had a chance to draw a bead on either of them. When he made it to the end of the pass, Clint looked back to see not only Con, but three more of Kinman's men rallying behind him. Turning to the trail ahead, Clint saw the terrain change back to the gravelly desert sand.

"We made it," Clint said while trying to catch his breath. The thrill of the charge had carried him through long enough and now his body was beginning to feel the strain.

Con's pawlike hand slapped against Clint's back. "Don't sound so surprised. I thought for sure you was going to take one from that goddamned sharpshooter back there."

"Guess I got lucky."

94

Shaking his head, Con said, "I seen lucky shots before and that wasn't one of 'em. Not by a stretch."

Clint was trying to come up with something to say that might cover his tracks. Before he needed to say anything, however, they saw Andrea standing off to the side of the trail amid a group of five of her men. There was still some shooting in the distance, but it had died down to just the occasional burst.

"Glad to see you two," Andrea said once they got closer. "I was hoping you'd make it out of there."

Clint walked straight up to her and felt the rage beginning to fester inside of him. If Kinman had been a man, she would have been knocked flat on her ass.

"Why didn't anyone tell me that the tournament started here?" Clint asked.

Still walking behind him, Con reached out to grab Clint by the shoulder and hold him in place. "Take it easy, killer," the big man said. His voice sounded more like that of a doting father than the second in command of a gang of killers. "It was my idea to keep you out of the know until we could be sure of you."

Clint spun around and clenched his fists. That was when he noticed that Con's hands were nowhere near his weapons. In fact, the big man didn't even look ready to dodge a punch.

"After what I seen," Con said, "I got no reason to doubt you. At least, not your skills anyway."

Andrea stepped in between the two men as though she spent the better part of her days preventing fights within her gang. Looking between them both, she said, "I take it our Mister Jenks worked out pretty well for a card player?"

"He ain't no card player," Con said. "That much I can tell you for certain."

Clint could feel his stomach start to tighten, but rather than let on to the others about what he was feeling, he backed away from Con and scanned a group of horses that had gathered nearby. He was more than a little relieved when he saw Eclipse among them. "As much as I'd like to continue this conversation," he said, "I'd feel much better once I put some distance between me and those damn rocks. Who do I have to thank for fetching my horse?"

"That would be me," came a voice from behind them all.

When he turned to look, Clint saw one of the other gang members that he'd seen doubling back around the back of the pass before any of the shooting had started. By the looks of things, he'd left behind a lot of his friends when making his way out of there.

Clint checked over Eclipse and saw that the stallion had made it to safety with nothing more than a few scratches. Those occasional bloody streaks in his coat had more than likely been picked up by being a bit too close to a few ricochets. "Obliged," he said while calming the Darley Arabian down with a few strokes of his hand along its mane.

"Forget about it. That sharpshooter you took out was keeping us pinned down as well. Another minute and we would've been caught in a cross fire. Least I could do was make sure that fine animal of yours got to meet you on the other side."

Clint swung up into the saddle and instantly felt better. Although he'd been trying not to think about it too much, he was planning on going back in for Eclipse once it was safer to ride through that pass. In the back of his mind, he'd been hoping that that decision wasn't going to cost Eclipse his life. He tucked his Colt into his belt because his gun belt had still not been returned to him.

"We still got some of our men fighting it out back there," Andrea said as she surveyed the pass like a field commander. "Who's going with me to make sure they get out of there in one piece?"

Clint could feel Con's eyes boring though his scalp like a pair of drills. He didn't need that incentive, however, to flick his reins and ride over to Andrea's side. After all, he still wasn't the kind to stand back and listen while others died for no good reason. For the moment, Clint didn't think of those men as outlaws and thieves. Instead, they were human beings who might die real quickly if he didn't pitch in and help.

"Just tell me where they are," Clint said. "I'll do my best to see to the rest."

"That's a mighty generous position for a lawman to take," Con said while fixing his eyes steadily on Clint. "Or maybe even a bounty hunter?"

Clint was too set in his frame of mind to let his cover story get shaken so easily. "Do you intend on baiting me or would you rather help keep some of your men from getting their heads blown off?"

Con tilted his head to regard Clint for another second before jogging over to the group of horses. Taking the reins of the first one he could reach, the big man climbed onto the animal's back and snapped the reins. The brown mare took off running and Eclipse was only a few steps behind.

Clint feared the worst when, as he got closer to the top of the rock formation, he could hear next to no shots being fired. That meant that the fighting was over and one side was dead. Steering Eclipse around a narrow path leading to the top, Clint thought about the time he could have spent helping some of these men rather than go back and forth with Con.

More than once, he passed a group of bodies laying strewn about like discarded toys. Since Con was in the lead, however, he followed the big man until they came to a stop on a spot overlooking the rest of the pass. Since the place was nothing but a shelf of dirty, sunbaked rock lined on two sides by a few medium-sized boulders, there wasn't much by way of places to hide. In fact, Clint's first reaction when he saw the top was to turn around and head back down.

But Con stayed where he was and hopped down off of his mount. Looking down at the bodies of several younger men that had been shot and left to bleed out, he stepped over to the side and looked down at the trail. "Those of you ridin' with Kinman can head on out and meet us," he shouted in a voice that sounded like roaring thunder. "And that includes any of you that was on the wrong side to begin with."

Clint spotted movement coming from behind one of the bigger rocks along the edge of the formation. After drawing his Colt, he jumped out of the saddle. A few steps brought him close enough to the rocks to see the pair of men laying behind them with their backs pressed against the stone.

"Come on out of there," Clint said. "It's all over."

Once again, Clint heard the booming roar of Con's voice. "It's all right, Jenks. They're some of ours."

Clint let out the breath that he wasn't even aware he'd been holding. The biggest danger with trying to pass for an outlaw was that he'd be expected to act like one. So far, he'd been defending himself and others, but there would come a time when he'd be expected to act without such lofty goals. He only hoped he could find a way to put an end to this mess before that happened.

Con was already back on his horse and making his way down the side of the rocks. "Bring 'em along," he said while hooking his hand over his shoulder. "The more the merrier."

Watching as the pair of men hurried around the rocks and started climbing down the side, Clint waited for the gang to clear off and give him a moment to himself. He made his way back to Eclipse and swung up onto the Darley Arabian's back. From there, he was at an even better vantage point than what was offered by being on top of the rocks. That extra couple of feet made Clint the highest point in the desert for at least a hundred miles in any direction.

Eclipse looked out over the desolate expanse and began fidgeting nervously while bobbing his head up and down. Clint could feel the animal's muscles twitching even through the layers of blanket and leather between them.

"Take it easy, fella," he said soothingly. "I'm not all that fond of heights myself."

Before allowing the stallion to get closer to the ground, where it belonged, Clint turned to look back toward the foot of the pass where he and Kinman's gang had ridden through what felt like an entire lifetime ago.

Clint was in no way surprised to see the group gathering there, straggling out with their tails between their legs to meet at a spot that was on the opposite side of the formation than Andrea had taken. More than anything, Clint wished he could have gotten his hands on the telescope Andrea had been using the day before, just so he could get a look at the faces of the Kinman gang's chief competition at this brutal tournament.

He knew those people gathered at the other end of the rocks had to belong to the Pearson faction since they'd seen no trace of the other gang on their way back into the pass. For the briefest of moments, Clint saw the sunlight glinting off of something shining at the front of that second group.

Tipping his hat in that direction, he turned Eclipse around and headed down to join the others.

TWENTY-THREE

Within the space of half an hour, all of the gang's men were gathered up and accounted for. Well . . . all the living ones anyway.

Bonnie Pearson stared through her spyglass to see if any of Kinman's men would bother coming back to collect their own. Next to her, Nelson sighted down the length of his Henry rifle and levered in a fresh round.

"One of them's poking around near the edge," he said. "I might be able to pick him off from here."

Bonnie gritted her teeth and watched as Clint rode up to the side and looked down toward her gang's position. "I see him," she said without taking her eye away from the lens. "Might as well let him go. No need calling down another round of fighting after making such a mess of this one."

She could hear the other man's reluctant mumble as he lowered his rifle. Still looking through the telescope, Bonnie almost thought twice about the command she'd given when she saw the smug look on Clint's face as he looked directly toward her and tipped his hat.

After collapsing the telescope between both hands, she dropped the instrument into one of her saddlebags and turned around to face what remained of her gang. "How many of us did they get?" she asked.

Nelson knew better than to try and make the news sound

any better than it was, so he instead faced her and said it straight out. "Five dead. Another six are wounded."

"Where are those six?"

Nelson pointed toward the back of the group and moved his horse aside so Bonnie could head that way.

Although the afternoon heat wasn't as bad as it could have been this far into the desert, the air was thick with pain and gunpowder. Every passing breeze reeked of spilled blood. As Bonnie made her way through her gang, she watched how the men looked at her, took in every twinge that pulled on the muscles of their faces.

While many of them looked scared and all were certainly shaken, there was no cowardice to be seen among any of them. Each man did their best to look square into their leader's eyes. They'd seen her set up the ambush and ride straight into the bullets as they'd started to fly.

Bonnie had been expecting some of them to change sides if she happened to lose this first battle, but the ones that weren't gathered in front of her were lying dead in the pass. Apart from a victory, she couldn't have asked for anything more.

She was at the back of the group now, looking down from her horse to half a dozen men passing around a bottle of whiskey and doing their best to clean their wounds using a single canteen of water.

"You men did me proud today," she said, even though she knew damn well what the outlaws were fighting for.

One of the men who'd taken a round through the rib cage, which had torn him up worse than the claws of a wild animal, gritted his teeth as clean water was poured directly onto his wound. The blood flowed out of him with the runoff, tainting the water dark red at first and then a lighter shade of pink. Finally, once the pain had died away, he sucked in a ragged breath and said, "You should'a told us."

"You're right," she said, nodding slowly. "You've all been with me long enough to know that I would never have dumped you somewhere to die without telling you exactly what you were getting in to."

The man who'd been pouring the water onto the other's wounds looked up from his messy task. "You said we were setting up an ambush. Them others came for a fight. They knew we'd be there. Hell, even a blind man could see that much."

Bonnie turned to face the entire gang. As soon as she did, she noticed that every eye in the group was already staring right back at her. Every last one of them were cold and steely orbs that had seen too much blood for one day.

"You're right," she said again. "This wasn't just some ambush. Kinman knew we'd be there just like I knew they would come to us. You all know about the tournament just like I do." Looking around, she saw them all nodding slowly. "Well, only the final round takes place in Rock Bottom, Arizona.

"This," she added while pointing over her shoulder toward the rock formation, "was the first round."

She had everyone's attention, but hadn't really said anything that really knocked them out of their seats yet.

"What happened back there was more of a test of my ability to lead than your ability to shoot. More important than killing every last man back there, each side was being tested on how well it held together under fire and how good each leader could perform under such harsh circumstances."

A ripple of uncertainty started forming within the gang, which spread throughout each of the gang members. It took more of a hold among the men who'd made it out without getting hurt since they didn't have any pain to divert their attention from what was being said.

"What are you telling us?" one of those men said. "I thought this was just a tournament."

"It is, but there's more at stake than just money," Bonnie replied. "This is about taking over Mondoza's business as well as his fortune and to do that, he needs to look for someone to lead in his place after he steps down."

A sudden, heavy silence descended upon the gang and settled over them like a shroud. This was the moment that Bonnie had been dreading more than any other. As soon as all of her men knew what was going on . . . as soon as they understood what Mondoza was offering, her life would be in danger from all of those that would rather have power than money. This was where ambition on the part of enough of her men could very well spell out her doom.

TWENTY-FOUR

"All of you who know me know that I would never have agreed to let you go so far without knowing what you were getting into unless there was so much at stake," Bonnie said almost pleadingly. "If I told you too much, we all would have been targets once we got closer to Arizona." Looking to Nelson, she said, "And that's because there's someone who works for Mondoza watching us all right now. Either from inside the gang or from a distance, that old man's got eyes and ears on us as well as the Kinmans to make sure that the rules are obeyed every step of the way."

Over the years, Bonnie had trained her eyes to pick up the slightest of details from people's faces whenever she spoke to them. Such training was unnecessary, however, to read the expressions of her men. Among the gang members, those that weren't thinking about making a play against her outright were too damn tired to do much more than go along with the ride that was already too far along to stop.

She looked over each and every face, making a note to herself as to which ones were the ones to count on and which she needed to make sure not to turn her back on. As she'd feared when she first thought about what would happen at this particular moment, there were just as many in one group as there were in the other.

"One thing that this means, however," she said while

keeping her eyes from betraying what she was thinking, "is
that this test wasn't set up as the first one without a reason.
It's meant to divide us, just like it was meant to divide
Kinman's men. And just because they were the ones that
made it through that pass, we can come out ahead by not
letting ourselves be divided. We can still make it through
this old man's bullshit rules and come out with his money
in our hands.

"We can stick together and take out the rest by covering
each other every step of the way until we're the only ones
left standing."

"And what happens then?" Nelson asked. "Are we supposed to start killing each other to see who wins it all?"

"That's up to you," Bonnie said with a razor edge to her
voice. "Personally, I've already started thinking of ways to
avoid killing my own men." Now, she turned back to the
rest of the gang, eyeing them with the same steely resolve.
"The same goes for the rest of you. I'm no fool. I know
what you're thinking and if you want to start moving
against me than there's nothing I can say that will stop
you."

Her hand moved to the gun at her side, hovering over it
and staying there without so much as wavering in the
slightest. She watched the others to see which one was
shifting on his feet just the right way . . . which one stared
at her with just the right combination of anger and confi-
dence and which one was responding to her the way a cor-
nered wildcat might respond to an approaching wolf.

"You," she said while staring straight at one of her men
who had been working his way up closer to her. "What do
you think of all this?"

The man she was looking at had been with the gang for
no more than a few months. He'd joined the gang after
gunning down a sheriff's deputy in Abilene. Ever since
he'd started riding with Pearson's crew, he'd been a good
man to have in a fight and had proven that worth more
times than Bonnie could rightly count.

"I think this all sounds like a load of horse shit," he said.

"I don't like being led by the nose. Not by you, not by anybody."

"That's why I told you all of this now rather than let you get killed off as we got closer to Mondoza's. You got a better way to win this thing, then I'm ready to hear it."

"You're talking now because you're scared we might all get smart enough to put you down and take all that money ourselves. You figure you can get some more use out of us if we stop a few bullets that should have been drilled into your own hide."

Climbing down off her horse, Bonnie stood with her shoulders squared and her eyes locked on her target. "Is that so?" she said in a fierce whisper that cut through the heated air like a dagger through soft flesh. "Then why don't you do this gang a big favor and take me out right here and now?"

"Because that lapdog of yours would kill me before I ever got the chance," he replied, motioning toward Nelson.

Indeed, Nelson was itching to get his hands on the man that she'd picked out of all the others. Nelson was always amazed at her ability to see right through to a man's soul and this was no exception. The timing couldn't have been worse to settle this, but it was too late to say so now.

"Yer damn right you son of a bitch," Nelson snarled. "I'll put a bullet in you before you even finish thinking about—"

"It's all right, Nelson," Bonnie said. "Stand back and let this man speak his piece. He was talking to me, not you."

As soon as it was obvious that Nelson was going to let Bonnie take care of this on her own, the man she'd been talking to went for his gun and pulled it free from its holster. He nearly got the weapon cocked before a single round tore through the air and dug a hole through his brain. He dropped straight back, leaving only a crimson mist to mark his passing.

"I've been tested enough for one day," Bonnie said while still holding her smoking pistol near her hip. "Anybody else care to try me?"

There were no takers.

She returned the gun to its place by her side without any flourish or with even the slightest bit of show. The motion was quick and simple, just like the one that had ended the life of the man speaking against her. Looking at the faces that were still turned her way, Bonnie noticed that much of the doubt had been wiped away.

"So what's the next part of the tournament?" one of the wounded asked her. "And where does it happen?"

"The next part is simple," Bonnie replied. "We get ahold of one of the people traveling alone to Rock Bottom and make sure they don't get there. As for the 'where,' it happens anyplace we find someone who fits that bill."

"Anyone in particular?"

"Mondoza's willing to pay for as many as we get our hands on. He'll pay more for the ones that are known gunmen, but he won't pay a cent for any brought in alive. I do have a target in mind," she said while turning toward Nelson. "Tell him what you told me."

Turning his single eye so that he could look over the gang, Nelson saw that with that one bullet, Bonnie had somehow wrested back control of every single one of those men. Now, it was time to reward them for making the right choice. "I got word back before we rode into Los Gatos that Clint Adams himself is making his way through these parts. We bring his carcass to Mondoza, and we might be rewarded enough that we won't even have to worry about winning the tournament.

"And I know how to find him," Bonnie said over the growing excitement of her men. "But I need to know that I can count on every last one of you. We need to work together if we're going to take down the Gunsmith. Is everyone with me, or are there still some of you who doubt me?"

It seemed as though the man that Bonnie had just killed was completely forgotten by every last member of the gang. As one, all of them raised their hands and gave a hoarse cheer directed at their leader.

TWENTY-FIVE

Clint had to let Eclipse run full-out before catching up with Andrea and the rest of her gang. When he made it back to her side and tried to tell her about catching a glimpse of the Pearson group at the other side of the pass, Andrea appeared as though she couldn't care less. Even though they were missing some of the men they'd started with, the entire gang seemed to be in good spirits.

"I thought you might want to know that the Pearsons are already re-forming and might even be ready for another fight before too long," Clint said.

Andrea shrugged and kept her eyes trained on the trail ahead. "Of course they'll be ready. If not, I would've been able to wipe out that whole group of back-shooting killers long ago."

"Can you at least tell me where we're going?"

"There's a town close to the border where we can rest up and get a hot meal in our bellies. After that it's on to the next round of the tournament."

"Which is?"

Even from where he was sitting, Clint could see Andrea rolling her eyes at him. She looked like a spoiled little girl who was relying on the effect she knew she had on some-one to get out of a punishment she so richly deserved. As much as he hated to admit it, the effect was not entirely lost on him.

"We're headed to Old Mexico," she said with a trace of exasperation. "You know that as well as anybody."

"And what's in Old Mexico?"

Andrea took a deep breath and let it out in a huff. "How come you're the one asking all these questions when my own men seem happy enough to just go along for the ride?"

"Because they're tired and fresh out of breath after fighting for their lives. They might have some more questions if you'd let them know what they're going up against."

"Are you playing my conscience now?"

"No. Just saying what's on my mind."

"Well whatever's on your mind can stay there for all I care," she said with a streak of anger tainting her voice. "You're damn lucky that I'm letting you tag along on this trip at all."

Now it was Clint's turn to be smug. "I'd lay good money on the fact that you had every intention of using me up at that pass back there. One more body to stop a bullet meant for one of your men will do just as well as another. Am I right?"

Andrea's face twitched slightly as though Clint's words had slapped against her cheek. "There's a lot at stake here and that means I have to do whatever's necessary to win."

"Even if it means letting others die for your cause whether they know what they're doing or not?"

"You did just fine back there," she said, turning on him with fire in her eyes. "And after what I saw you do in that pass, this speech really doesn't seem to hold a lot of water. You killed a man yourself . . . unless you've forgotten already."

"And now that I've proved myself, I guess that means you've judged me worthy to live." Clint kept his tone calm and steady since that seemed to have more of an effect on Andrea's resolve. "Now, instead of using me for cannon fodder you decide to use me as another one of your killers. Sounds like your father may have been right all along in setting up this tournament—it's made you into a perfect little murderer."

For one of the few times since he'd met her, Andrea looked every bit of the killer that someone in her position should be. When she glared at Clint, she looked poised on the verge of drawing on him right then and there.

"Go ahead and do it," Clint whispered. "Make your father proud so you can ride into Arizona and take over the family business. You'll be able to murder a lot more people once you're in his shoes. That's what you want, isn't it?"

"I'm only after the money."

"That's right. Once you get that money after killing . . . how many more people?" Clint rubbed his chin as if he was trying to figure the number. "Hell, it doesn't matter. Once they're dead, you can take that money and ride away to live a nice happy life. Is that the plan?"

She had nothing to say to that. The silence that hung between them was almost a solid, living thing. It stabbed cold fingers through both of their bodies and stole the breath right from their mouths. Andrea turned away from him and rode on, letting the silence brew until something had to give.

"You did a good job back there," she said finally. "But don't let that go to your head. One thing you've got to remember is your place in this gang." Turning toward Clint, she added, "You have no place in this gang. The only reason you're here is because you came in handy once. And as long as you're helpful to me and my men, you can stay. If we win that money, I'll even cut you in for a piece of it.

"But remember that if you become more trouble than you're worth, I'll see that you won't be found until hell cools off. Do you understand me?"

Clint watched her speak and noticed how the rage was kept to a smoldering minimum behind her eyes. She was speaking as a professional now, which was exactly what he'd been trying to push her toward the entire time. Each time he'd spoken out of turn or antagonized her had been for the sole purpose of seeing if she was truly the leader of this gang.

Even as he watched her fight back at the pass, Clint wasn't sure if it was Andrea or Con who was the leading force behind the gang. Seeing as how Andrea was Mondoza's daughter, that would explain how she could get a group like this together. But actually leading it was a different story all together. Now that he'd gotten her to tell him what was going on, Clint had had a chance to read her expression just as he would if he was still sitting across from her at a poker game.

"You know something?" he said. "I believe you just might be able to pull this off."

It took a moment for her to set her anger aside. Once she did that, confusion was the next thing she felt. Shaking her head, it was all she could do not to start laughing at him. "Just when I think I'm about ready to punch your face in, you say something to change my mind. Do you do this to everyone you meet, Jenks?"

Clint thought seriously about that question for a moment. "Actually . . . yes. Just about, anyway."

"Well, I kinda like it. Keeps me on my toes." She fixed him with a playful smirk for a second and then looked forward at the miles of desert stretching out before them. "Con says you've got more to hide than just a fake name."

"Really?"

"He says you're a lawman or—"

"Or a bounty hunter? Yeah, he told me that one, too."

"I think there's something to it."

Clint hadn't actually expected his fake name to carry him this far without any questions. That was why he rarely went through the trouble of using one. But his own poker face held up, and he merely shrugged the words off. "Okay. If I said you were under arrest, would you come quietly with me?"

She leaned over so she could speak softly into his ear. "You should know by now that I don't come quietly at all. That's not any fun."

"Then I think I'll stick to being who I am. I never did

have much of a desire to wear a badge anyway." It was always easier living a lie when it was at least partly the truth.

"I don't care who you are," she said. "Half my men have never told me their real names either. Just keep working like you did today and you'll always be welcome with us."

"And what if I did turn out to be the law?"

Andrea drew her shoulders up and turned her face toward the sky. She trembled as though she'd just caught a chill and said, "Mmmm, that means I shared my bedroll with a keeper of the peace. The thought of doing something that dangerous and foolish makes me want to pull you off that horse and give it another go."

Watching the way Andrea looked at him and listening to the husky tone in her voice, Clint knew that she was dead serious. The strangest part was that, after all the sneaking around and close calls he'd had over the last few days, Clint was actually starting to feel the same thing toward her.

Suddenly, all he could think about was the feel of Andrea's skin and the taste of her lips. He had things to do when they got to town, but after that, he planned on paying Andrea another visit. After all, there was no reason to get some pleasure out of this self-appointed mission he'd taken on.

TWENTY-SIX

By the time they pulled into the town, the gang was too tired to think about much of anything besides putting up the horses and then finding a place to get a drink. Clint was right with them on that account. After all, the trail wore the same on everyone. Despite the constant reminders he was giving to himself, he couldn't help but feel a kind of kinship with these men.

It only made it harder to focus in on why he was truly there when the men started letting him into their circle. Sitting around a small table in the back corner of a saloon, Clint, Con and several others enjoyed their food and drink while telling each other highly exaggerated stories about places they'd been and things they'd done. Before he knew it, Clint was telling his own stories as well, making sure to change just enough so that some of the more famous events weren't recognized.

"So what the hell made you come all the way from Los Gatos to join up with a bunch like this?" Con asked while motioning toward all the others who'd gathered around.

Clint actually had to think a moment to get beyond the story he'd already had prepared to answer that question. It took him a few seconds to get the true goal of diverting a possible gang war to a place where the fewest possible innocents could get hurt in mind. A few seconds more, and

he reminded himself about possibly doing damage to one
of the biggest criminal leaders in this part of the country.

At first, all he could think of was what he was supposed
to say. And it was at that moment that he realized how a
man could live his entire life in a gang like this. It was one
of the few lifestyles that came equipped with its own set
of morals, its own code of honor, its own rules and its own
system of justice.

Clint was far from actually chucking everything and sign-
ing on with Kinman, but for the first time he felt as though he
could truly understand those that did. When he turned toward Con and the others, he had to picture them as the sum
of their deeds rather than the men sitting at his table.

It was easier to lie to a group of killers and thieves than
to people you knew by name. But they *were* killers and
thieves, he reminded himself. With that firmly in mind,
Clint spewed out some story about getting his hands on
some of Mondoza's money and putting a bullet into a few
of his men as well.

There was only one problem that he could see, however.

Con wasn't buying any of it.

"I saw the way you handled yourself today," Con said.
"And I ain't never seen no card player fire a gun like that."

"Guess I just have a knack for it. I spent some time in
the army, as well. That sort of thing sticks with you no
matter how hard you try to shake it."

All the men gathered around the table seemed to have
heard more than enough of Clint's stories. Already, they
were moving on to bigger and better tales about some job
they'd all pulled in Texas. Clint excused himself and got
up to get some time in the cool desert night that he'd come
to know and appreciate.

The air inside the saloon was dirtier than the floor. Pun-
gent smoke hung like a thick fog weighed down by stale
breath and the scent of cheap alcohol. Compared to that,
the air just outside the saloon's door had been blown in
straight from the heavens. It was clean and crisp, settling
around Clint like a welcome embrace.

Glancing around at his surroundings, Clint realized just

then that he didn't even know the name of the town he was in. It was just some wide spot in the road that offered a better place to sleep than the ground. Beyond that, it could have been anywhere. Clint looked up at the stars and made some rough calculations as to how far he'd traveled in the company of outlaws.

"Clearin' your head a bit?" came a voice from the saloon to interrupt Clint's train of thought.

Clint spun around and got a look at Con, who was closing the door behind him. "Yeah. All that smoke starts getting to me after a while."

"Same here." Con gripped a bottle half-full of whiskey in his left hand. "Just wanted to get a few words with you before you wandered back to Andrea's room for the night. Sometimes she's not all too picky about the company she keeps."

"I'm not quite sure how to take that," Clint said, feigning an offended tone. "Would that be an insult against me or her?"

"You know damn well what I'm saying." Con's voice had gone from an amiable conversational tone to the cold, threatening chill that would normally come seconds before somebody found himself dead.

Clint braced himself for the moment he'd been waiting for ever since he'd decided to come along with this group. When he spoke this time, he dropped all the changes he'd made to his own voice in order to make the character of Marcus Jenks. It wasn't much, but it was enough to make his entire bearing shift over to that of the real Clint Adams. "You got something on your mind," Clint said, "then you should probably just spill it."

"It's already common knowledge that you're not who you say you are. Andrea doesn't think it's much of a problem, but that's where we differ."

"If she's the leader of this outfit, than what you think doesn't mean a whole lot, does it?" Clint knew better than that, but he tried taunting the big man to see which way he would jump.

"She don't know shit, boy," Con said with a snarl tugging at his upper lip. "Whatever I do, she'll back me. And right now, I'm asking you a few questions. Answer them good enough and I'll be happy. Once I'm happy, Andrea stays happy."

"Just shut up and ask your questions."

"Where'd you serve in the army?"

Clint knew that one was a mistake the minute it slipped from his mouth. Rather than try to bluff his way through unfamiliar territory, he simply hardened his gaze and stared back at Con.

"How'd you know to come after us right now?" the bigger man continued. "And what made you think you could get away with trying to play all of us for fools?"

Listening to the way that Con asked his questions rather than the actual words themselves, Clint knew that whatever answers he gave would not be enough to satisfy the gunman. He'd already been judged in the bigger man's eyes and his sentence was already decided. Clint knew there was no way out of this for him.

No way but one.

"I don't need to hear this," Clint said. "Not after all I've been through today. You got a problem with who winds up riding with your gang, take it up with your boss. I'm tired of listening to your voice."

And with that, Clint turned and walked away from Con with quick, steady steps.

Even as he made his way across the street and headed for a nearby corner, Clint kept his ears open for any and every sound he could detect. What he would hear in the next few moments could very well decide who walked away and who would be buried in this small, unknown town.

Clint listened for the sound of a gun being drawn.

He listened for a hammer being cocked or even that machete slicing through the air.

But all he could hear was the cool desert wind blowing around his head and the sound of footsteps trailing closely behind.

TWENTY-SEVEN

Clint picked up his pace, making sure not to walk too fast so as not to give the man behind him too much to think about. He knew that Con was following him and had a pretty good idea of what was on the bigger man's mind. After all, it wasn't too hard to figure out. That was the good thing about outlaws. They wore their hatred on their sleeves.

The town they'd chosen for the night wasn't big enough to have a good or a bad side to worry about. In fact, the only thing Clint was worried about was running out of town altogether. He'd only led his shadow less than a block and a half and already the streets were beginning to thin out into sparsely built-up trails marked by rotted wooden planks set roughly next to each other in a row.

Rather than do Con a favor by walking straight out into the pitch blackness of the desert, Clint hung a sharp right and walked around one of the buildings on the outskirts. As soon as he ducked in off the street, Clint pushed his back up against the side of the building and waited for Con to walk by.

As soon as Clint stopped and waited for Con to stick his head around the corner, every sound he'd been hearing simply stopped. There were no more footsteps and no more traces of anyone following in his tracks. It was as though the sounds themselves had been swallowed up whole by the sands of the desert.

Clint stood by and waited for a few seconds until his instincts told him that he'd waited for too long. There were times when quiet was a peaceful, beautiful thing. This most definitely was not one of them.

Already, Clint was beginning to curse himself for allowing things to make a turn in such a bad direction so quickly. If Con had wanted to kill him, he would have wanted to be in a place exactly like this. Somewhere he could pull the trigger and dump the body without leaving much of anything that needed explaining to Andrea. And rather than head for safer ground, Clint had walked straight into a killing field. He knew better than to commit such a potentially fatal mistake.

He should have known better than to get involved in this whole mess to begin with.

Suddenly, a subtle noise snapped Clint out of his thoughts. It came from around the corner, but could never be confused for a footstep . . . especially the footstep of someone the size of Con. The sound came again, only this time Clint recognized it for what it was.

It was something tapping on the side of the house.

A ruse to get him to look around the corner and put his own head in the noose. Clint knew he might have made some mistakes this evening, but he wasn't about to make another one. But then again, it would have been rude not to go where he was invited.

Taking a step forward, Clint made sure to scrape his boot along the gritty earth so he could make as much noise as possible. From there, he moved around the corner while ducking down onto one knee, barely keeping his head low enough to avoid the bottle that was swung his way to smash against the edge of the building.

Bits of broken glass fell down upon Clint's head amid a spray of backwashed whiskey. Striking with his left hand, Clint sent a sharp jab into Con's stomach, which knocked a good portion of the air from the bigger man's lungs. While Con reeled back a step to try and clear the haze from his eyes, Clint got to his feet and sent a quick knee down the same path as his fist.

The combination of one blow coming after another was more than enough to send Con reeling. Doubled over in pain, he still managed to keep his hold on the broken piece of the bottle, which was exactly what Clint had been hoping to break.

"You just proved my point," Con wheezed between strained breaths.

"You've been looking for a reason to go through with this, so let's see what you make of it." Clint threw himself back a step to avoid the jagged glass that Con swung toward his chest. "If I wanted to hurt any of you I could've done it at the pass."

But Con wasn't listening. All he could hear was the voice of the man he meant to kill and the sound of his heart pumping sheer aggression through his veins. He pulled the broken bottle in close to his body and stooped over into a defensive fighting stance. From there, he began circling Clint while twisting the bottle menacingly to catch his opponent's eye.

Clint kept his hands open, ready to block or grab Con's next strike. He could feel the Colt swinging at his side and knew he could get to it in less than a second if he decided to end this fight that much quicker. But the gun reminded him of something that needed to be said before taking this thing too far.

"If you were so suspicious of me," Clint said, "then why give me my bullets back there? Why not just let me stop a few rounds and then leave me to rot alongside all the others?"

"Wasn't my choice," Con replied while stabbing straight out with the bottle.

Clint twisted to the side and went to grab Con's wrist, but the other man muscled out of the hold before quickly turning around to face him.

"Andrea?" Clint guessed.

"You got that right." Another quick swipe, but only to keep Clint moving rather than draw blood. "She seems to have taken a shine to you. Told me that she knows damn well that you ain't just some card player." This time, he lashed out with the bottle and twisted midway through the strike to twist the jagged glass up toward Clint's face. The razor-sharp edge caught Clint in the upper part of his chest and dug a bloody trench through his flesh.

The pain Clint felt was like a bucket of cold water splashed onto his face. It didn't feel good, but it woke him up and sharpened his senses. Ignoring the warm trickle of blood coursing through his shirt, Clint waited for Con to follow up with another swing. Clint then twisted Con's body inside his arm until Clint was close enough to reach down and snatch the machete from Con's belt.

Clint kept right on moving until he was behind the other man, with the big blade in his right hand. He then shoved Con roughly, forcing him off his balance and watching as he spun around to take one more wild swing with the bottle.

As soon as he felt Clint go by him and even steal away his blade, Con could think of nothing more than slicing open Clint's throat and burying that bottle deep into his flesh. He spun around in a fast half-circle, leading with the jagged glass. The bottle cut nothing but air, however, and once his arm was extended all the way after his swing, the cool steel of the machete was pressed against the side of his neck.

"You don't have to do this," Clint warned. He held the machete to Con's jugular and pushed in just enough to make sure he had the big man's attention. "Walk away now and don't come back. Otherwise, you don't leave me any other choice."

Con's eyes darted from Clint's face to the machete and back again. Making his choice, his face hardened and he let out a defiant snarl. He brought the bottle straight up toward Clint's midsection, putting every last bit of his strength behind the crude weapon. The first thing he felt was the blade cutting so quickly through his neck that he didn't even have a chance to hurt. When the pain did come, it wasn't in his throat, but lancing through his hand and knuckles.

Clint could tell just by looking into the other man's eyes that Con wasn't about to give up just yet. At the first sign of movement, he took half a step back and brought the machete down to cut through Con's hand, severing four of his fingers right where they sprouted from his hand.

The bottle fell to the ground next to the pile of freshly harvested digits. Con's mind was so awash in pain that he couldn't even get out the scream that churned inside of him and fought so desperately to escape. Running on pure instinct, his other hand went for his gun, but once again the machete was just a little faster.

Clint was certain he'd done enough damage to slow the big man down. But when Con refused to drop and even made a clumsy grab for his pistol, Clint responded by raising the machete over his head and bringing it down. The blade whipped through the air and sliced through toughened hide like it was nothing more than thin cotton. There was a slight tearing sound and then the heavy thud of something hitting the ground.

Con's eyes widened and his teeth clenched together in expectation for the agony he thought was coming. He saw the blade move and heard the results, knowing in his heart that when he looked down, he would see his hand laying near his feet.

"Just remember," Clint said as he raised the blade up so Con could see it, "I gave you the chance to walk away from this."

As much as he didn't want to, Con looked down at what had dropped onto his boot. Instead of another piece of his body, he saw his pistol, still wrapped in its leather holster sitting there amid the glass and bloody fingertips. At that moment, the part of his holster that was still wrapped around his waist fell off of him and dropped to the ground.

Now the pain from his mauled hand began chewing into Con's flesh. That, combined with the shock he'd been given turned his world into a sea of black. He tried to say something, but he was already drowning.

Clint caught the big man and lowered him down to the ground. "Sorry about that, big man," he said to the unconscious outlaw. "But this sure beats the hell out of being dead."

TWENTY-EIGHT

The confrontation with Con was just what Clint needed to clear up his notions about what it was he was doing and get him back on track. Rather than try to figure out all of what was happening, he realized he simply had to accept the fact that this tournament was much bigger than he'd thought going in and that he just needed to find a way to make that work to his advantage. Otherwise, all of his efforts had been for nothing.

An entire lifetime behind a badge couldn't even put him where he was at the moment. From where he stood, he could see two gangs of outlaws and god knows how many solo gunmen lining up like ducks in a row, making a trail all the way to Tito Mondoza himself. The federal authorities would be able to do a world of good if they just knew where Mondoza lived. On top of all that, Clint had the chance to pull apart the two biggest gangs in the area.

That was why he was here.

Not to get to know how Kinman and Pearson thought or even what they'd been up to. Clint needed to stop them, plain and simple. Diverting his attention for too long had only tipped his hand to the wrong person, and nearly got him killed.

It was time to get back to business.

Clint thought about all of this as he dragged Con's unconscious body across the street where he could prop it up against one of the darkened storefronts. He looked for any trace of a doctor's office, but could find nothing that was marked as such. In a town this small, he doubted any of the stores needed to be marked at all.

Once Con was situated, Clint ran back to the saloon and got the attention of the barkeep. He pulled the scrawny, dark-skinned young man aside where none of the rest of the gang could hear what they were talking about.

"Is there a doctor in town?" Clint asked.

"Sí, Doctor Lopez."

"Where can I find him?"

"I can call him for you, señor."

"No," Clint insisted. "Just tell me where he is. I'm not feeling too good."

The bartender looked nervously between Clint and the rest of the drunken gang members. Deciding not to ruffle any of the wrong feathers, he nodded and motioned for Clint to follow him outside the saloon. "That house on the corner," he said, pointing out the correct place that was less than twenty yards from where Con was lying in the shadows.

"Thanks." Clint pulled a dollar from his pocket and pressed it into the bartender's hand. "This is for keeping your mouth shut about this. Don't tell anyone . . . especially not any of my friends. As far as they know, I came out here to ask about finding a woman for the night."

"Sí, sí," the younger man said. "I understand."

With all the rest of the gang either at the saloon or the hotel on the other end of town, Clint was able to get Con over to the doctor's house without raising suspicion in too many people. The doctor, on the other hand, was plenty suspicious.

The town's doctor looked to be in his early sixties with a head full of bushy gray hair. He kept his mustache well trimmed and even at this time of the night, he seemed to be dressed for a night out. "What on earth happened to his hand?" he asked.

Clint did his best to carry the gunman inside and onto

one of the beds. "He had a little accident cutting firewood."

"Is that what you two were doing across the street? Cutting firewood? From here, it looked like you were trying to kill each other."

"You're half right, I guess," Clint said. "I was hoping not to kill him."

The doctor reached over to a beaten rolltop desk and retrieved a pair of wire-framed glasses. He carefully looked over Con's hand and clucked his tongue like a worried hen. "Gonna have to take the rest of the hand," he said finally. "You might have saved him some pain if you'd have finished the job."

Clint looked around the small house. "He didn't exactly give me a lot of time to think. Besides, shouldn't you be trying to save as much of him as you can?"

The doctor's lip curled up and he looked like he was about to spit on Con's face. "I've seen plenty like him come through here. They steal what they want and give me plenty of business before moving on to Old Mexico where they can escape the law. I should let this one bleed to death."

"I'd appreciate it if you didn't. At least, not until I leave. I'd like to think I did some good by not running him through."

The doctor walked slowly to another room and came back with his hands full of bandages and a needle and thread. "Oh, you did plenty of good, señor. I suppose you'll want him ready to travel after the rest of your friends sleep off the liquor they spent all night drinking."

"Actually, I had something else in mind." Once again, Clint looked around to see if there was anybody else within the small dwelling. "Does your family live here also?"

"My wife, but she's too sick to leave her bed. If you're thinking of robbing me, I'd save you the trouble. My last patients took all I had a few nights ago after I tended to one of their gunshot wounds. Probably friends of yours."

"I doubt that," Clint said. "Actually, I wonder if you could get me some rope?"

The doctor's face turned pale and he began backing away. "R—rope?"

Holding out his hands, Clint shook his head. "It's not for you. It's for him," he said while pointing to Con. "He'll be waking up soon and I need to make sure he doesn't give you any trouble until we can get him into a jail cell."

Suddenly, the old man looked as though the sun had found a way to shine through the night and illuminate his face alone. "Are you here to arrest these men?" he asked hopefully. "Are you with the law?"

"Not exactly, but I am trying to put this one and the rest of his gang away. But I need your help."

"Anything, señor. Anything I can do, I will do."

"First . . . the rope."

The doctor nodded and dashed out through the back door, moving faster than Clint thought a man of his years could go. When he returned, he was carrying a length of rope that was so dirty and blackened that it might have been taken from a well bucket in the man's own yard.

"Is that going to hold?" Clint asked. Looking over to Con, he noticed that the outlaw was just beginning to stir. "Never mind. Hand it over and you see what you can do about his hand."

The two worked pretty well as a team. The doctor tended to Con's wounds while Clint trussed him up like a rodeo calf. When he was finished, Clint stood to one side and watched as the doctor carefully went about his work.

"Here," Clint said while taking out some money. "This is for your trouble."

"No, señor," the doctor replied while shaking his head. "You're a good man doing a big job. This is my part to help. And don't worry," he added before Clint could say anything else. "I'll keep him quiet until your friends are all gone. It's a small town. I'll know when it's safe."

Clint held on to the money and then set it down onto the doctor's desk. "Then consider this as payment for what was taken from you last week."

Only looking up from his task for a second, the doctor regarded him with a warm, kind face. "*Gracias, señor. Muchas gracias.* Before you leave . . . can I know your name?"

"Clint Adams."

It felt as though it had been years since he'd even heard those two words out loud and strung together. Once they were past his lips, they hung in the air and charged Clint's spirit back up to full capacity. He felt as though he'd found himself once again.

Marcus Jenks would not be missed.

"Thank you, Mister Adams," the doctor said after adjusting the glasses on the end of his nose. "What you've done to this one alone is enough to deserve a reward that I cannot pay."

"Then you know him?"

"Sí, sí. This group comes through here many times before. The rest usually camp outside of town."

"The rest?" Clint asked. "How many more?"

"There's usually a dozen or so that come here and twice that many that sleep in the desert."

Clint thought for a second. As far as he could remember, he'd only heard of the Kinman gang being no more than ten, or maybe thirteen men at a time. Any more than that would have been another complete gang. "Do you know if those others are here now?"

The doctor was silent for a while, busying himself with the stitches. Although Con seemed to be making more noise and breathing heavier, the doctor didn't seem to pay him any mind. "I'm no scout, but usually where there's one group, the other is not far behind."

Clint nodded and then pat the doctor on the back. "I've got to leave. Thanks again."

He left the doctor to do his work and ran to get Eclipse. If his hunch was correct, he wouldn't have to ride for long before finding Pearson and her gang.

TWENTY-NINE

The best part about being in the desert was that there wasn't many places for someone to hide. Clint rode Eclipse back along the way the gang had come in from the trail, and quickly spotted the winking traces of campfires no more than a mile or two in the distance.

Since the blackness of night was nearly as complete as a velvet curtain that had been draped over the sands, he made no attempt to conceal his approach. Besides, he didn't have time to let Eclipse ride any slower than a full run and he wasn't all that interested in keeping his visit a secret.

Once he got within a quarter of a mile of the flames, Clint strained his eyes to pick out any trace of a greeting party. Unfortunately, the darkness that had been his ally was working just as hard for the other side and he didn't see the approaching horses until he was almost on top of them.

Both Clint and the other riders were charging forward in order to gain some semblance of surprise. Both of them succeeded.

Clint brought the Darley Arabian to a halt and let the others close the distance between them. When they got close enough for him to see that they'd drawn their guns, he raised his hands to either side and put on his best innocent look.

"I just came out to talk," Clint said while there was a rider coming slowly straight at him and two from either side. "There's nobody else with me."

"I can see that," came a voice that wasn't half as rough or threatening as the one Clint had been expecting. In fact, the voice was smooth and most definitely female.

The horses were all breathing heavily after their run and when they took a few more cautious steps closer to Eclipse, they combined to form what Clint imagined it would sound like if the desert itself had a set of massive lungs. The men on either side were each pointing pistols at him. The one in front came in a bit more, giving Clint a good look at a slender, pale face outlined by a wispy mane of hair.

"You're the one that's taken to riding with Kinman's bunch," the woman in front said.

Clint nodded. "And you're Bonnie Pearson. I'd like to have a word with you if I may."

"Is that so? Why should I have anything to say to you after you took up arms against my men?"

"If you don't like what I have to say, you've still got one less gun to worry about in the tournament. I'd say that puts me at the disadvantage here, not you," Clint pointed out. "Might as well hear me out since you've got nothing to lose."

Bonnie looked from Clint to the men that were positioned on either of his sides. After a nod from her, they backed off a step, but still kept their guns aimed at him. When she nodded again, they both cocked their hammers back. "I'll listen, but if you so much as look toward that gun of yours, both of my men will fire. Nobody's fast enough to hit both of them. Not even you."

Clint reflexively checked the position of his two guards. They'd moved their horses a little behind him so they could fire at the same time, if need be, and not worry about hitting each other. He had some ideas for getting out of there if he had to, but none of them were good enough to wager his life on. Hopefully, he wouldn't have to do anything so desperate.

"You've been following Kinman's gang," Clint stated. "Even since before all of this started."

Bonnie didn't move. Even in the near total darkness, her eyes managed to catch the stray beam of moonlight and reflect it back to the men. "So, what concern is that of yours?"

"I guess I just don't see the point in it. After all, if you two don't get along so well, then why not try to conduct your business away from each other? That seems like it would be better for both of you."

"You came all the way out here to tell me this? Maybe you should peddle your advice to Kinman. She's always up for a good lesson. So if you've got a point, now's the time to make it. I've got other things to do."

"Actually, I did come here for something else," Clint said. "I thought I might test out a theory of mine that concerns you and Tito Mondoza."

"Go on."

"I'm thinking he's taken to hiring a pretty rough bunch to look after his firstborn."

Although Bonnie's expression didn't change in the slightest, her posture and the flicker of emotion in her eyes shone through the darkness for anyone practiced enough in the art of seeing such things. And after all his years of looking for hints just like those at the card table, Clint was a master artist in that regard.

"You two can go," Bonnie said to the men flanking Clint. When they hesitated for a moment to look doubtfully back at her, she spoke again with more of an edge in her voice. "Take his gun if it makes you feel any better. But once you've got it, clear on out of here and let us talk in peace."

Clint didn't like it much, but he grudgingly allowed the man on his right to reach out and snatch the Colt from his belt. With a casual glance, he memorized every line in that man's face so he knew where to go if he needed to reclaim his weapon.

Once both men turned their horses and rose back toward the fires, Bonnie slowly drew her gun and pointed it in Clint's general direction. "Why don't you climb down off of that horse? I'd feel better talking to you face to face."

Hesitating just long enough to let her know that he wasn't one to jump when commanded to do so, Clint took his time climbing off of Eclipse's back. Seconds after his boots hit the sand, Bonnie dismounted as well, keeping her gun loosely in hand.

"All right," she said. "You know something more than most, so go ahead and spill it. That's what you came for, isn't it?"

"I know exactly how important Andrea Kinman is to Mondoza. And I have a pretty good feeling that you're something more than just another participant in this joke of a tournament that he's holding."

"Joke?" Bonnie scoffed. "Five of my men are dead and plenty more are wounded. You think that's a joke?"

"I'll bet it is to Mondoza. Every one of those dead men is one less in your gang. And the smaller your gang is, the less he has to worry about. He's thinning the herd of those who would want to take over his position. Surely you must see that."

"I do. But it's not his position I'm after. Just his money."

"Is that why you hired yourself out to keep an eye on Andrea? Maybe even steer her in the right direction now and then?"

Stepping up close to him, Bonnie held her gun just low enough to press it against Clint's midsection. From there, she ran the barrel lightly up his chest and traced it over his neck. "That's what I was just about to ask you, Mister Adams. By the way . . . how much did it cost Mondoza to put the high and mighty Gunsmith on his payroll?"

THIRTY

Clint stood with one hand resting on Eclipse and the other hanging down where his Colt ought to be. Hearing Bonnie call him by name was a pleasant surprise since that meant that he wouldn't have to bother with too much unnecessary double-talk and verbal sparring. But there was still one thing that bothered him about her knowing since, as far as Clint could remember, he had never actually met her before in his life.

"Do I know you from somewhere?" he asked.

Bonnie smiled and looked up at him. From this distance, the red in her hair showed up like a faint watercolor tint around her face. "No, but I know you. Or, at least I've heard enough about you that I feel like I know you."

Stepping back a few paces, she kept the gun pointed at him, but not so he thought he was in any immediate danger. She regarded him the way she might look at a prize steer. "Clint Adams," Bonnie said as though she was quoting scripture. "Tall, handsome type who rides alone and carries a Colt revolver. Heard one of my uncles say that you used to travel on a fine black gelding. Whatever happened to that horse? Or was that just a mistake in the telling?"

"No mistake," Clint said. "Duke had to be put out to pasture."

"Happens to the best of them." Bonnie stepped up closer

again, this time keeping the gun pressed lightly against his side. Reaching up to touch his chin, she ran her fingers over his skin and onto his face. "But it was the scar that gave you away," she said, gently touching the thin, pale streak cutting down his left cheek.

"I heard you were in the area and had been keeping my eye out for you. When I spotted you with Kinman's bunch, I thought you just looked like Clint Adams. But . . ." She paused just long enough to pull his face down so she could touch her lips against his. When she spoke, her breath slipped inside Clint's mouth. ". . . when I saw you in action, I knew you were the real thing."

Clint took a second to soak in the moment. Her body was thinner than Andrea's, but Bonnie moved against him with a slow, serpentine rhythm that triggered an instinctual need for her deep within himself. Strands of her hair caught the occasional breeze and tickled against his skin. Suddenly, the desert night didn't seem so cold.

"You got the answer to your question," Clint said. "Now how about the answer to mine?"

Bonnie moved her face just enough to touch her lips to Clint's skin and brush along the whiskers that sprouted from his chin. Still keeping the gun against his side, she used her other hand to feel the muscles in his back, causing a little smile to play across her thin, pink lips. "You were right," she replied. "Mondoza hired me and my gang to make sure that Andrea didn't decide to go off on her own. We've butted heads plenty of times in the past, but she's not that hard to figure out. In fact, I've used her for several of my jobs."

"And I don't suppose she knew about how helpful she was to you?"

"She just might have, but since both of us were getting what we wanted out of it, we've kept up our little relationship."

"So your rivalry is just a clever front, I suppose?"

Bonnie smirked and let the tip of her tongue trace along Clint's lips. "That's real enough. Even the best relationships have their rocky spots."

Wrapping his arms around her trim waist, Clint decided

to take full advantage of the woman's talkative mood. "And what is it, exactly, that you two get out of all this?"

"I get a whole other gang to use as my scouts and step on all the tripwires for me, which clears the way for my boys to ride in and take the jobs she didn't bother with. Having two gangs in the area tends to get folks jumpy. Once they get rid of one, they think they're safe for a while."

"Which is when you come along and pick up her leftovers."

"More or less."

"How does Andrea get anything out of that?"

"She gets to run her own little group of two-bit thieves and make a living out of defying her daddy. I think she knows well enough how everything's set up. She's not stupid, after all."

Clint pulled her in closer until he could feel Bonnie's firm breasts pressed up against him. She let out a little gasp under her breath, but allowed herself to be handled. The gun, however, stayed right where it was.

"So if you're working for Mondoza, how come he's making you go through with the tournament? Like you said, you lost some of your men when they could've gotten their money just the same without fighting in that pass."

"We're still in the tournament. The money I'm making watching Andrea is extra."

"Let me guess," Clint said as he brushed his lips along the outer edge of her ear. "You figure you can get nice and close to the old man when you're making your last report on his daughter."

Bonnie's laugh was both deadly and alluring. In it, there was no trace of deception or remorse. "You got that right. His days are numbered and he knows it. Those are the best kind of rich men. He's doing everything but slipping the noose around his own neck."

"And you don't think he's setting anybody up? You think he just assumes all of you killers will play fair and take the prize he gives you?"

Now, Bonnie dug the fingernails of her free hand into Clint's back while taking a quick nip out of his neck. "I'm not stupid, either, Clint. I don't appreciate anyone treating me like that."

The little punishment served its purpose as a way to both warn and excite him. "Now," she said in a soothing whisper, "the only thing I need to know is why you're here."

"I want to get a look at Andrea's competition."

Bonnie raised her eyebrows and nodded slightly. "Oh really?"

"Mondoza's giving out a lot of money. I hear this next part of the tournament is a scavenger hunt. A man can probably retire to the good life by cashing in on that part of the contest alone."

"I never heard of the Gunsmith working for rewards like that."

"Three hundred thousand is a lot of money. All I want is a piece of it."

Bonnie looked at him as though she wasn't quite sure what to think of what he was telling her. It was obvious that she wanted to believe him. But whether or not she actually did was anyone's guess.

"You work for me and I can see that you get a bigger piece than you might have anticipated," she said as her hand slipped down his back and then onto the top of his thigh. "But how do I know I can trust you?"

"Believe me, I could care less if either of you gets rich in this stupid contest. All I want is a nest egg that I can retire on after my riding days are over."

"If I'm taking the chance of letting a spy into my camp, I'll need more than your word to prove that you mean what you say."

Clint's hands drifted up over her hips and brushed the sides of her breasts. Her skin felt smooth yet firm and she took in a deep breath when his fingers slid gently over her nipples.

"Come with me into town," he said. "And you'll get all the proof you need."

THIRTY-ONE

Clint was still outside the town limits when he started to hear the first shots ringing out from the middle of the small settlement. The popping explosions rang up into the quiet desert night and spread out in all directions. Once he and Bonnie had ridden down the single street bisecting the entire town, Clint could also hear shouting voices followed by screams and more shots.

"Sounds like your friends are keeping themselves busy," she said.

Clint's eyes narrowed as he flicked Eclipse's reins. After talking to the doctor about what the gangs usually did when they were here, he had a pretty good idea that they would be up to their same tricks. He'd hoped that they would have kept themselves busy drinking long enough for him to get back and prevent some of the damage.

Without waiting to hear more screams, Clint turned Eclipse toward the saloon and headed off down the street. Bonnie was close behind him and when they arrived at the small building, they were just in time to catch a fresh round of lead as it punched several fresh holes through the wall.

Before dismounting, Clint turned to Bonnie and held out his hand. "I need a scarf or bandanna."

"Catching a chill?"

"Just let me borrow whatever you can spare."

She lifted her hands to her throat and unfastened the top three buttons of her jacket. When she pulled it open, Bonnie revealed a dark blue bandanna tied around her neck. Once it was removed, she exposed a man's thin cotton undershirt that was cut for someone twice her size. The neckline curved to expose the top half of her breasts and clung to her as though it was made out of liquid. Bonnie bent forward to hand him the bandanna, giving Clint a view of her small, shapely curves and hardened nipples.

Clint took the bandanna, folded it diagonally and then tied it around his face. Hopping down from the dark stallion, he felt like the villain from a cheap, yellow, back novel.

"Need any help?" Bonnie asked.

Clint stood facing the door to the saloon. His pistol was still back at Pearson's camp and so he reached behind him for the rifle slung to Eclipse's saddle. "No," he replied. "I can do just fine on my own."

Shrugging, Bonnie said, "Suit yourself." Then she watched as Clint turned and pushed open the door.

The saloon was filled with pure chaos. Every bit of available space was filled with bodies, bottles, gun smoke, flying chairs or thrown glasses. Nobody inside the place even noticed that Clint had walked in, which was just fine by him. The first thing he did was take a few steps away from the door and windows since those seemed to be the primary targets for people looking to shoot up the place. Next, he looked about for any familiar faces.

At a glance, he picked out no less than half a dozen of Kinman's thugs, although Andrea herself was nowhere to be found. Her gunmen, however, were gleefully laying waste to the saloon as well as anyone that happened to be in it. It wasn't so much of a fight as a whirlwind of havoc that tore through that bar. The next thing for Clint to do was throw himself into it headfirst.

In need of a starting point, Clint stepped toward the first scream once he was in sight of the gang members doing most of the damage. One of the killers he'd seen only once before the battle at the pass shoved down a woman dressed in a red dress decorated with sequins and fringe. The woman hit the floor hard on her side and when she looked up, she saw the outlaw coming down toward her with his fists balled up, aiming for her face.

Clint was reacting before he even got a chance to think. He cut through the tangle of bodies and flying objects to throw himself at the killer only a second before the man was able to knock in the woman's face. Making contact with his shoulder, Clint barreled through and took the gunman clean off his feet before slamming him down to the floor.

The woman had both her arms raised to protect her face and was too terrified to lower them, even when it was obvious that the blow was not going to be coming. Rather than move, she curled her body into a defensive ball and screamed into her arms.

Clint wanted to stop and help her get out of the way, but there was still too much to be done. Looking around, his attention was caught by two more of the gang members lifting the bartender up from behind the bar by both of the terrified man's arms. With a chorus of booming laughs, the gang members picked up the small Mexican and dropped him onto the bar, smashing a row of shot glasses in the process.

One of the gunmen started reaching for the whiskey bottles, but the other made a grab for the cash register.

"Hey!" Clint shouted, as he worked the lever on his rifle.

Both of the gunmen turned at the sound of his voice. Seeing the mask before anything else, they stopped and regarded him with no small amount of confusion. "Who the hell is that?" asked the one going for the cash.

"The man holding a rifle on you," Clint replied. "Now step away from the bar and get the hell out of here."

Both men looked at each other once before going for their guns. Both gunmen moved with impressive speed. Impressive, that is, for a couple of drunks.

Clint had plenty of time to raise the rifle to his shoulder, aim and take a shot before either man got a chance to fire their pistols. His bullet caught the man nearest to the register high in the chest, spinning him around and sending him to the floor. The other gunman who'd been concentrating on torturing the barkeep cleared leather, but had been shaken up enough for his aim to be completely blown.

Not wanting to waste all his ammunition, Clint surged forward and grabbed hold of the rifle as though it was a steel club. The barrel was hot in his hands after just being fired and rattled within his fist when he cracked the stock against the side of the gunman's face.

More shots exploded within the saloon, this time all aimed at Clint. The gang members doing the shooting were also screaming obscenities toward him, but their words were lost amid the detonating gunpowder. Clint turned to get a look at them, making sure to move deliberately and efficiently.

The main thing separating the living from the dead in a gunfight was the ability for a man to keep his wits about him when the lead started to fly. Although Clint was outnumbered and outgunned, he took the time to crouch down and pick his targets while the other three shooting at him simply squeezed their triggers as many times as their fingers would allow.

THIRTY-TWO

Clint's main objective was to take these men out of the tournament, killing as few as possible along the way. With his right hand, he tossed the rifle up and grabbed it by the firing grip. In another flick of his wrist, he snapped out the lever and spun the entire weapon around in a tight circle, which chambered another round. His left hand was then free to reach out and snatch up the pistol belonging to the man he'd just knocked out and he brought that gun up to bear on his new set of targets.

One of the gang members, a younger kid who was still new to the group, locked his wide-eyed stare on Clint and brought his hand up to fire. The other two were more practiced in getting out of these situations and did the first thing they could think of by grabbing the closest innocent bystander they could see.

Clint acted without having to think. The younger gang member was scared and probably the least efficient with a gun, but he was also the one getting ready to fire. With only a slight adjustment in his aim, Clint shifted the rifle toward the kid, squeezed the trigger and turned back toward the remaining two without pausing to see the results of his shot. All he needed to hear was the crash of a body going to the floor through a bunch of nearby chairs and tables.

One of the two remaining gang members was doing his

best to hide behind the petite frame of a small blonde woman. He nearly lifted her off her feet in his attempt to get a better shield. The gun in his hand was trembling slightly as he looked between Clint and his fallen comrades.

"Let the woman go and you might just live through this," Clint said once he saw the gang member wasn't even aiming in his direction.

The man pulled his trigger and sent a shot twenty feet to Clint's right. At first, Clint didn't allow himself to be distracted. But then he heard the agonized scream of someone at the bar and his first impulse was to look and see who'd been hit.

Clint forced his eyes forward, however, and blew the gunman off his feet with one rifle shot that whipped over the woman's head and straight through the gunman's eye socket. Before he could allow himself to see who'd been wounded, Clint turned toward the last gang member in the place.

"You don't get a warning," Clint said while levering in his last round.

Although he'd been trying to keep hold of an older man who'd been playing poker, the gang member wasn't having much luck. After seeing what just happened, he simply let go of the old man's shirt and tossed his pistol to the floor.

"Con's gonna kill you," the outlaw said with a foul sneer on his face.

Clint stepped forward and held the rifle's barrel to the man's forehead. "He's already tried his luck. Didn't do much better than you." And then, with a twist of his upper body, Clint brought the rifle's stock around in a quick half circle to smash the wood against the killer's skull.

The gang member stayed on his feet, quickly blinking his eyes for about two seconds before falling over like a bottle from a fence post.

Once he was sure there were no more gang members to be seen, Clint turned to get a look at who'd taken the stray bullet. Sitting against the bar, clutching his blood-soaked shoulder, was the Mexican bartender.

"You all right?" Clint asked after hurrying over to the man's side.

"Sí, sí. I was thinking I'd be dead before you came in. Thank you, señor. Thank you so much."

Clint turned to look back at the folks who'd been chosen for hostages. The old man was standing guard over his former captor while the woman was already sitting in the farthest corner of the saloon. Someone was crouching down beside her, gently rubbing her shoulder and speaking softly to the petrified woman.

It was Bonnie.

Once he was close enough to hear what was being said, Clint held back and let Bonnie deal with the woman. After all, it seemed as though the younger girl was more scared of him than the leader of the Pearson gang.

Bonnie pat the girl on the cheek one more time, stood up and then turned to face Clint. "She's fine," Bonnie said. "Just a little shaken, is all."

Nodding, Clint looked over his shoulder at the old man who appeared to be getting ready to start kicking his downed captor. "These men need to be tied up and taken to the law," Clint said as the old man was rearing back for his first strike. "Well . . . two of them anyway. Can you see to it?"

The old man looked up at Clint and nodded fiercely. "Yes, sir."

"Is there law in this town?"

"Not as such, but we got someplace to hold 'em until a marshal passes through in a week or so."

"Good. Need any help?"

"No, señor," the bartender said. "You've done plenty. We can clean up."

Clint looked around and was convinced that the gunmen who were still breathing would be no threat to anyone until they woke up in several hours. The people in the saloon looked more than anxious to get their hands on the gang members. Nodding, Clint began walking toward the front door. "Fine," he said. "I'll keep the others away from here as long as I can, but you'd best be quick about it."

Bonnie followed him out, not saying a word until the saloon's door closed behind them. At that point, she stood and faced him with her arms crossed over her chest, regarding him with a mix of confusion and admiration.

THIRTY-THREE

"You mentioned something about proving something to me?" Bonnie said.

Clint nodded. "I'd say I made my point pretty well."

"And what point was that, exactly?"

"That my loyalties don't lie with Kinman or any of her men."

"Is that supposed to make me trust you?" she asked. "Especially when you might just decide to cut me and mine down just as quickly if the mood struck you?"

"I didn't say anything about trusting me," Clint pointed out. "I could care less if you trust me or not. I just wanted to be sure that you knew I wasn't on Kinman's side. Especially with the tournament in full swing and all."

Suddenly, Bonnie's face lit up as though she'd just walked in front of a burning torch. "Ahhh," she said. "So this all just boils down to money." Looking at him a little harder, she fixed her eyes upon Clint and squinted slightly as though she was trying to draw him inside her mind. "Or is it about power? If it's not one, it's always got to be about the other."

Clint heard approaching footsteps coming from the other end of the street. Even in the middle of the small town, the darkness of the desert was absolute, making it difficult to make out any details of who was coming besides the fact that they obviously didn't care who knew they were there.

Once they got a little closer, the voices started to soften just a bit as the ones speaking noticed that they were no longer alone on the street. Hoping that neither of them had been recognized yet, Clint lowered his face and headed toward a nearby alley. While not as concerned about hiding herself, Bonnie followed him in between the buildings.

The additional shadows within the alley swallowed both of them up like minnows inside a whale's mouth. When the talkers got close enough, they looked right into the alley but were unable to see more than a black gaping maw. From where he was, Clint could make out the faces of two more of Kinman's men all but looking straight at him. They stood there for a second, squinting into the blackness, but then shrugged and moved on past the saloon on their way to the hotel.

Bonnie seemed more than a little amused at Clint's behavior.

"What?" he asked in a quiet voice once the others had moved along.

She stepped up close to him, using the sound of his voice as her only guide. Bonnie held her hands out in front of her. When they brushed against Clint's chest, she moved in so that their bodies were just close enough to touch. "I think it's funny that you even bother trying to hide from those oafs when you took down three of them back in that bar without even breaking a sweat."

"In case you forgot," Clint replied, "I never got back my gun and that rifle doesn't do anyone any good without any shells."

"You could've found a way."

Her hands worked their way over his chest and down his body, fingers gently probing the lines of his muscles beneath his clothes. Her voice had become an excited whisper that was like a warm breeze in the dark desert air.

"You wanted to take them out of the tournament," she reminded him. "So that means you want to side with me. Is that it?"

"There's something else I need from you."

Bonnie caressed Clint between his legs, cupping the growing hardness there. "That's funny. I was just about to say the same thing."

Clint forced his mind to keep to the matter at hand; it was a battle that his body was not about to let him win so easily. She seemed to know exactly where to touch him, exactly how hard to rub and long to stroke. Just then, he could only think of one thing he needed from her as his hands began to do some probing of their own.

Bonnie drew in a sharp breath as she felt Clint's fingers slip between her legs. Even through the thick material of her jeans, the warmth of her body was easy enough to find.

Once he could tell that Bonnie was no longer the only one being pushed by her desires, Clint was able to wrest a bit of control back from her expertly moving hands. "What I did in the saloon was to prove to you that you don't need your gang. We don't need anybody else but each other to win that tournament."

At once, Bonnie's hands, heart, breath and body came to a stop. Her eyes caught a glimmer of moonlight that had somehow managed to push its way through the narrow space between the two buildings' roofs. She looked up at him with undisguised excitement. "You mean go to Arizona with just the two of us?"

"From what I hear, most of the others will be traveling alone anyway. This way, we still get an advantage of being on a team and only have to split the money two ways rather than ten."

For a few moments, Clint thought that Bonnie was about to push him away and maybe even walk back to her horse. The silence between them was thick and crackling with tension. Her eyes hung in place like two ghostly shimmers and Clint could almost see the furious flow of thought going on behind them.

"So what else do you need from me?" she asked.

This, Clint knew would be the moment that would decide how the rest of this entire thing would work out. If she responded well enough, he might just have a shot at not only cutting the gangs down even further, but striking at the source of this whole blasted tournament without even having to go there himself.

If she responded badly, on the other hand, he might be less than a second away from feeling something else pressing against his body. Something like the barrel of Bonnie's gun.

"What I need," Clint said, "is Tito Mondoza."

THIRTY-FOUR

At first, Clint couldn't hear anything in the darkness of the alley. Then, after a few moments, he could just make out the subtle sound of Bonnie's laughter rattling quietly in her throat. She was so close to him that he could feel the vibration of her chest against his as she reacted to what he'd just said.

"Is that all?" she asked. "I thought you'd want something that might be hard to get. But Mondoza? Sure, I'll just have my boys go and get him tomorrow morning."

Clint's hands roamed freely over her body. Responding to the slight motions of her hips and the patterns of her breath, he kept his touch lingering over the places she liked, stroking her until she needed to lean against him for support. "It's not like that," he whispered. "All I need to know is where he is."

"I told you. The place is called Rock Bottom, Arizona."

"Yeah, but *where*? Is he in a ranch? A house? A mansion? Is it in town? I've heard about Mondoza, but I've never known exactly where the man is. I never even heard of Rock Bottom until a few days ago."

While listening to him speak, Bonnie had had enough time to collect her thoughts and get over her initial reaction to Clint's request. Now, her mind raced with other things.

It worked to balance out what she wanted to do and what she thought she should do.

Sensing this, Clint said, "I know you can tell me because you've dealt with Mondoza in the past. Besides," he added while brushing his lips against the smooth skin just below her ear, "I can't work with Andrea. She's too close. You're different. You know a better deal when you see one."

"I also know who I'm really dealing with," she said, almost as though she was talking to herself.

Her mind was turning toward his way of thinking, Clint knew. He could feel it.

"What are you going to do with Mondoza that you couldn't do at the tournament?" she asked. "He'll be there."

"We both know that Mondoza's got plans going on beyond just setting up a tournament and then sitting back to let the best shooter win. You're living proof of that. If I can get ahold of him . . . alone . . . I know I can persuade him to rethink his plans so that we come out of this on top. Besides, with me in the tournament, he knows damn well that half the outlaws he wants to see there won't even show. Most of them have probably already tried and barely gotten away with their lives. The last thing they want to do is face me when I'm looking for a fight."

Bonnie's hands had begun sliding beneath Clint's clothes to rub over his bare skin. She wriggled in his grasp as he talked softly into her ear, grinding her hips wantonly against his. "You know something, Adams?" she said. "Coming from anyone else, that would sound like the biggest load of self-centered bullshit I've ever heard. But what gets me more than anything is that you're probably right about all of it."

Just then, her hand drifted between his legs again. It stayed there, working him until Clint's hard shaft filled her grip. "You know something?" she whispered into his ear. "That night you were with Andrea . . . I was watching you two. I saw what you did to her. Saw how you fucked her and it was all I could do not to rush down there and join in."

THIRTY-FIVE

Clint started to say something, but before he could get the words out Bonnie was sliding down his body until she settled onto her knees in front of him. Her hands worked at the front of his pants, unfastening them and then working his penis free of the clothing. When her hands found his bare skin, Clint was overwhelmed by the rush of sensations that she lavished upon him.

Her fingertips probed gently down his shaft, touching him softly and then teasing him with the ends of her fingernails. Before he knew it, he was leaning back against the wall, reaching down with one hand to hold her by the back of the head just in case she tried to move from the perfect position she was in.

But Bonnie wasn't going anywhere. Working her lips over the head of his cock, she flicked her tongue in and out to take fleeting tastes of his skin before gently placing him inside her mouth. She sucked hard while taking him in, running her tongue all the way down to the base of his shaft. When she pulled her head back, she made sure that her lips were just barely touching him, which sent waves of tingling pleasure all the way through Clint's body.

"Does it make me a bad person to get so worked up after seeing what you did in that bar?" she asked in a naughty whisper. "Because ever since the first time I heard about a man called the Gunsmith, I've wondered what it would be like to feel his cock in my mouth." She moved forward, sliding her mouth over his rock-hard penis and wrapping her lips tightly around. Bobbing her head back and forth, she made loud, wet noises as she savored the feeling of him inside her and relished the way she could make him harder and harder until his hands were locked tightly onto both of her shoulders.

Clint looked down to see Bonnie's red hair blowing in the wind, fluttering against his naked lower half. Seeing her crouching there with her legs bent and spread apart while she worked her mouth furiously on him made Clint want her even more. Every time she devoured his length, he could feel the tip of her tongue running along the bottom of his cock, teasing him all the way up and back.

When he could feel his pleasure coming to a climax, he reached down and pushed her back. It took a lot more strength than he thought and she seemed genuinely upset at being denied the feel of him between her thin, soft lips.

"What are you doing?" she asked as he grabbed hold of her arms and lifted her to her feet. "Why did you make me stop?"

Clint held her firmly, but was careful not to be too rough. With just the right amount of force, he moved her across the alley until it was her back that was pressed up against a wall. When she made contact with the dirty brick, she let out a breath that was part grunt and part gasp. Her eyes went wide with an excited gleam.

While tearing open her pants and pulling them down around her ankles, Clint locked his eyes with hers and said, "You know damn well what I'm doing. It's what you wanted while you were watching me and Andrea." Her underclothes were made of thin cotton that was damp with her moisture. The flimsy garment tore away easily when Clint ripped it free.

Bonnie pressed herself against the wall, holding her arms out to either side as though she was trying to grab onto the bricks and hold on for the ride. After kicking her pants off and tossing them to the side with a quick twitch of her ankles, she wrapped one leg around Clint's waist and thrust her hips out until she could feel his cock sliding between her thighs.

In the inky darkness of the shadows, Clint couldn't even see all of the woman's body. Part of her face was hidden by the night while the rest stared back at him hungrily. While moving his hands over her sides, he looked down to see himself disappear in the nearly complete darkness. What he felt, however, told him more than his eyes ever could about each and every one of Bonnie's slender curves. Even though he couldn't see how she twitched in response to his probing touch, he could feel her flesh grinding against him and pressing tightly into his embrace.

The warmth between her legs felt so good against Clint's skin that he almost resisted when Bonnie reached down to fit him in between the lips of her pussy. That reflex gave way to another desire, however, which he didn't even try to fight.

With a quick thrust of his hips, Clint drove himself deeply inside of her. Bonnie responded by wrapping both arms tightly around his neck and tightening the leg that was curled around his waist. She moaned softly into his ear and when he slid out to pound into her even harder, she needed to bury her face in Clint's neck so her cries could be muffled by his naked flesh.

Both of Clint's hands were working their way down until he could cup her firm little backside and feel her body clench with every thrust. The next time she was pushed up against the wall, she hopped up to wrap her other leg around Clint's waist, entwining it with the first so she could be completely supported by his hands. Every muscle in her body writhed in time to Clint's pounding hips. Every breath she took was expelled in a passionate moan that was stifled only by his skin.

Blinded by the curtain of red hair that had enveloped his entire face, Clint could see nothing that wasn't a part of Bonnie. Her pale skin shimmered less than an inch from his eyes, surrounded by the shimmering mist of crimson. Her arms were locked tightly around his shoulders. Her legs laced securely about his waist and the lips between her thighs tensed in a quick, trembling pulse as waves of pleasure surged through both of their bodies.

Some part of Clint's consciousness was aware that there were other people walking down the street beyond the alley. Although he was fairly sure that they were too deep inside the shadows to be seen, Clint wouldn't have been able get himself to move even if they were in the middle of the street. In his ear, he could hear Bonnie's ragged breathing form into roughly whispered words.

"Somebody . . . somebody's out there," she said.

Her body became still, but she only slightly let up on the pressure she was using to hold on to him. Sure enough, Clint heard the sound of passing footsteps and a pair of strange voices engaged in a conversation.

Still unable to see much of anything through the darkness and Bonnie's hair, Clint moved his hips slowly between her legs and eased his shaft up inside her moist vagina. When he was inside her as far as he could go, Clint slid out and then pushed in again, grinding back and forth before thrusting inside with one quick push.

Overwhelmed by the motion of Clint around and inside of her, Bonnie felt the first hints of a powerful orgasm that was about to push its way through every inch of her flesh. She'd already felt the ripples surge through her once already and now that they were coming back, they seemed even more powerful than ever.

Rather than cry out like she wanted to, Bonnie sunk her teeth into Clint's shoulder and gnawed on him while grinding herself against his rigid penis.

Clint thought he was about to break the silence as well, but figured he'd be able to keep himself under control. When he felt Bonnie's orgasmic writhing and felt her teeth press into his flesh, that control was put to the test, the strain of which was eased by the fantastic way her pussy clenched around him as if to massage the base of his cock.

Finally, the passersby moved on and Clint thrust into her one more time. As soon as their hips slammed against each other, he exploded inside of her in a burst of passion that made it difficult for Clint to keep his footing.

Once he was able to catch his breath, Clint said, "So how about it? Are we in this together?"

"You drive a hard bargain, Clint Adams," Bonnie said as she eased her feet back down to the ground. "My gang's not gonna like it, but what the hell. I can always buy another one."

THIRTY-SIX

The first thing Clint saw when he made his way back to the hotel was a very angry Andrea Kinman waiting for him in the room they were sharing. She was wearing the clothes she'd had on earlier in the day and even the dirt from the trail was still clinging to her face.

"Where's Con?" she asked with a hard edge in her voice.

Clint went to his pile of belongings and fished out some more ammunition for his rifle. The empty holster at his side felt to him as though he was missing a limb, but he knew that problem would be solved soon enough. "I must have missed the part where I was assigned to be the man's keeper."

"Then I suppose you don't know anything about our men that were gunned down at the saloon, either?"

Clint's face reflected just enough surprise to be convincing. At least, that was what he'd been shooting for. "How many? When did it happen?"

"I just heard about it," she said while studying his face carefully. "The locals already cleaned up the mess, but I know at least two are dead. There's more being held in what they use for a jail, but I don't think Con is one of them."

Clint knew this would be an important moment for his plan to either work or fail. As much as he'd tried, however, there simply was no real way to prepare for it. Just like in any honest poker game, all he could do was be ready to think on his feet and do the best with what he'd been dealt.

"Actually," Clint said hesitantly, "I saw Con not too long ago."

"I know that much. Go on."

"He tried to kill me."

Although Andrea's expression gave away a bit of anger, there was no surprise. "And what happened? Did you get to him first?"

"No . . . Pearson did."

This time, there was definitely surprise written all across her features. "What? That's impossible."

"He came after me because I caught them both . . . together. I wasn't the only one who saw them, either. I think there were some of your men passing by an alley on the other side of the saloon a few hours ago. They saw the same thing I did. Con and Pearson carrying on like a couple of dogs in heat right there in the open."

Andrea's eyes narrowed as her mind chewed on what she'd just been told. The way she looked at him told Clint that she did not believe all of his story. For his plan to work, however, she only needed to believe some of it . . . just enough to disrupt the flow of things.

"Who else saw them?" she asked.

"Hard for me to say. I was at one end of the alley and they were at the other. I'm pretty sure it was one of yours, since the locals seem to have hidden themselves away and your boys are the only ones strutting about like they own the place."

Andrea began walking toward him, every step she took draining away more and more of the harsh lines that had been etched across her skin. Once she was within arm's reach, she grabbed Clint by the lapels of his jacket and pulled him toward her. "I've been hearing some nasty things about you, Mister Jenks."

For a second, that name didn't strike much of a chord in Clint's mind. Before he made a mistake, however, he remembered his fictional identity. "You don't need to call me that anymore," he said.

"My, my. You just keep rolling out the surprises tonight, don't you? What should I call you then?" Still keeping herself close to him, Andrea stood on her tiptoes and put her mouth up against his ear. "Maybe I should just call you Gunsmith like everyone else."

Upon hearing that name, Clint felt more relief than anything else. "Why didn't you start that earlier if you knew about it the whole time?"

"Because I didn't know until earlier today. Con told me. It seems he recognized you from somewhere, but just couldn't quite put his finger on where. Turns out that he ran across you some time ago in Amarillo. I told him to keep his mouth shut about it until I decided what to do with you."

Clint's hands stayed at his sides. His body remained motionless. Only his head turned slightly down to get a better look at her as his eyes roamed her face for any signs of danger. "And what have you decided?"

"I think you'd be more of a help to me if you didn't bother hiding your name during the tournament. It'll give us an edge that nobody else could possibly have."

"And what about Con? Are we going to take care of him and Pearson all in one strike?"

Andrea turned away from him and stalked over to the other side of the room. Her head was lowered and her muscles were tensed like those belonging to a jungle cat circling its prey. "I need to make sure about Con." Reaching toward the door, she pulled it open and stuck her head out into the hall. "Mike! Joshua! Get in here!"

Within half a minute, two of her gang came striding into the room, moving with enough speed to please her, but not so much as to make her think that they were jumping at her command. Outlaws were like that, Clint knew. Always worried about how they looked to the other animals that they were around. Always fighting for dominance within their pack.

"You two were at the saloon earlier tonight," she said,

standing in front of them with her hands held at her sides near her gun. "Where was everyone else?"

The one who'd answered to Mike asked, "You mean before those bastards shot up the place?"

"That's right."

"Yeah. We were there. Then we patrolled the rest of the town just like you ordered."

"Did you see anything else while patrolling? Anything . . . unusual? Like in an alley, perhaps?"

Both of the men looked at each other and then looked at the floor to hide the sneering grins that had slid onto their faces. "Yeah," Mike said. "We heard someone fuckin' in an alley about a block away from the saloon. It was after the shooting, but they wasn't on the run."

"Why didn't you see who it was after all that happened at the saloon and all?"

"We was on our way to the saloon and when we got there and saw the bodies, we checked out the area, starting with them in the alley. But by the time we got there they was done and . . . and gone."

"Did you gather up all the rest of the gang like I asked you?" she asked.

"Yes."

"And how many showed up?"

"There's us and four more."

Andrea looked anything but pleased with that news. "Get the hell out of here," she said with a dismissing wave of her hand.

The pair turned slowly and left the room, talking amongst themselves as they stepped into the hall and shut the door behind them. Once she could no longer hear their voices or footsteps outside, Andrea turned back toward Clint wearing a smile that could only mean one thing: trouble.

"I think I just figured out what I'm going to do with you."

Clint didn't even bother trying to hold back his laughter. "Oh really? Now that you know who I am, why should I care about what you think or say anymore?"

"Because no matter what you call yourself, you still decided to come along with me for a reason. And since we're
still both interested in the same thing, I don't see why we
can't still work together."

"Ah yes," Clint said. "The tournament."

"Don't take me for a fool, Clint. I know that tournament
is just my father's way of killing off anyone stupid enough
to try and play along with his little game. I'm talking about
the money."

Moving in so that he was close enough to see the flecks
of silver in her eyes, Clint put both of his hands upon her
hips and said, "Now I've got a question for you. How do
you feel about splitting that money two ways instead of
ten?"

THIRTY-SEVEN

Clint didn't need to talk for very long to convince Andrea to go along with a plan that was roughly the same as the one he'd struck with Bonnie. Even so, after all that had happened during the last twenty-four hours, Clint was more tired than if he'd walked all the way across the desert. His mind was exhausted from trying to keep up with all the different angles he was playing as well as keeping tabs on all the players he was dealing with.

What had started out as a simple idea to infiltrate a gang and chew it up from the inside had become something much more than that. Now, there was over half a million dollars at stake along with enough power to control all the major criminal activity on this side of the Rockies.

As soon as his head hit the pillow, he felt as though his entire body had been dropped off a cliff and was toppling end over end through empty space. Andrea left him alone so she could work things out with her men, which didn't do any good for his nerves either. Rather than let himself get any more worked up about all the possible ways for this mess to work out, Clint settled into a chair in the corner of the room with his rifle across his lap and his hat over his eyes.

Somehow, he managed to get a few hour's sleep.

*   *   *

The first light of dawn felt like a burning ray of fire when it fell upon Clint's eyes. It made him jump from his sleep with a start as though the morning itself had crept through the window just to sneak up on him. His first instinct was to try and be as quiet as he could manage since he wanted to get out of the room without attracting any attention. But when he took a look around while working some of the knots from his muscles, Clint noticed that there wasn't anyone in the room to disturb.

Either Andrea had already gotten a start on her day or she'd never come back to the room the previous night. Either way, Clint didn't like the fact that he didn't know exactly where she was. If he'd been a superstitious man, Clint would have felt this day had started off hexed.

He did feel better when he saw that he still had his rifle and that it hadn't been tampered with while he was asleep. Nearly every part of his body let him know how dissatisfied it was after having spent the night in a hard wooden chair, but by the time he'd made it down the stairs and out of the hotel, Clint managed to find plenty of more important things to worry about.

For starters, he wanted to get his Colt back from the Pearson camp outside of town, as well as his gun belt back from Andrea. Having spent the night in a well-maintained stable, Eclipse seemed more rested than his rider and took off like a shot when Clint climbed into the saddle and gave the reins a quick snap.

The ride to the outlaws' camp was less than two miles long and by the time he got there, Clint's stomach was doing flip-flops inside of his ribs. The smell of coffee and bacon cooking over open flames drifted through the air, beckoning him toward the largest gathering of men as though the rising smoke had been spelling out his name.

Clint drew Eclipse to a stop and hopped to the ground, walking casually over to Bonnie, who just happened to be standing near the largest fire. As soon as she saw him, Bonnie separated herself from the rest and waved him over to a more secluded spot away from the others. Before Clint could walk up to her, he noticed her pointing toward one of her men, who turned and started heading toward where she was standing.

"Glad you came out here," she said once Clint and the other gang member were about the same distance from her. "Saves us the trouble of coming into town after you."

Suddenly, Clint wished he'd taken the rifle with him instead of leaving it hanging from Eclipse's saddle. Pretending to ignore the other man headed toward them both, Clint said, "I've got some news for you. It's about the matter we were discussing last night."

Bonnie didn't say anything. Instead, she simply stood with her hand resting on the handle of her gun while regarding Clint with a watchful eye.

The sound of approaching footsteps crunched against the sand behind Clint, drawing closer with every passing second. They stopped once they were directly behind him. When he heard the distinctive noise of a gun being dragged against leather, Clint spun around, ready to lunge forward and either swing his fists or try to snatch the gun from his attacker's hand.

The other man was holding a gun, but not with the barrel pointed at him. Instead, Clint found his own Colt being presented to him handle-first by the wary gang member. Once the Colt was slapped into his hand, Clint relaxed and shrugged apologetically to the outlaw. In response, the other man simply turned and walked away, giving Clint and Bonnie their privacy.

"I don't think we have to worry about Kinman," Clint said. "Her gang took a heavy hit last night, so she's ready to look for a new strategy to win the tournament. We talked things over last night and she seemed—"

"Gone," Bonnie interrupted. "She and the rest of her crew pulled out of town a few hours before sunrise. I know all about it."

Clint felt his gut twist into an angry knot. How could he be so stupid? He'd been in such a hurry to get out of the hotel and away from town that he hadn't even tried to look and see where the rest of Kinman's men had gone, or even if they were still at the hotel at all.

"But don't worry," she said calmly. "We've been busy this morning. In fact, we just got back before you showed up."

"Early risers, huh? What kept you so busy?"

Bonnie looked toward the main fire and sniffed the fragrant air as though she was taking a leisurely stroll around her very own kitchen. Then a darkness drifted over her face and seeped all the way into the tone of her voice. "As soon as my scouts saw Kinman's group pulling out, we chased them down and got them to join up with us. Well, most of them anyway."

"I take it the rest are . . ."

"Oh yes," she said with a curt nod. "As doornails."

Clint nodded slowly as his mind did its best to wrap around this huge turn of events. If the picture had been narrowed down to only one gang, and an even bigger gang at that, it would make stopping them that much harder. "And what about Andrea?" he asked.

Pointing past the cooking fires, Bonnie drew Clint's attention to a small cluster of people gathered at the edge of the camp. He'd seen them there before, but hadn't paid them any mind. Now, as some of the gang members walked away, he could see the huddled figure of Andrea Kinman sitting in the sand. Her arms and legs were hog-tied, which made it that much harder for her to even keep herself sitting upright.

"We're rolling straight into Arizona," Bonnie said, raising her voice enough to draw all the eyes in the camp her way. "Fuck the rest of this tournament. Mondoza wants to see who's strong enough, who's smart enough, ruthless enough? He's just got to look our way. He's just got to look at who comes riding straight up to his front door with his own daughter held out as a sacrificial lamb.

"And all we've got to do is ride through every town we pass and every camp we come across like a goddamn thunderstorm! We were supposed to go to Old Mexico to bring back some of the men that had been running from Mondoza or even some of them that would hunt him. To hell with that and to hell with the rest of his rules! I say we burn a trail through these states and grab everything we can along the way.

"Starting here," she said while pointing toward the town in the distance, "we steal whatever ain't nailed down. By the time we knock Mondoza off his throne, we'll be too big to worry about the law and too powerful to have to answer to anyone ever again!"

At once, the entire group of outlaws raised their fists, their guns, even their forks into the air and let out a rallying cry. Clint could feel the air cracking with the hunger for blood as though it was static lightning raking across his skin. Their eyes were wide and when they shouted, they all bared their teeth like a pack of starving coyotes. The instant Bonnie snapped her fingers, a group of her men jumped onto their horses and tore off for the town.

In his mind, Clint could already hear the screams that would be coming from that town as soon as those men got there. When he blinked, he could see the fires that would be set and the bodies that would surely be left behind. Bonnie then turned to him and flipped open her coat to reveal the holster strapped around her waist. Already, the desert's heat was making itself known and a fine layer of sweat was glistening on her body. Clint couldn't help but think about the night before when his hands had been over every inch of that body.

THIRTY-EIGHT

"You wanted to prove yourself to me the other night," she said. "You did a hell of a job, but things have changed now. Way I see it, Gunsmith or not, you're in one hell of a bind right now. I snap my fingers again, and all these men pull their guns and make themselves famous. Or . . . you can pass one more test and ride into Arizona with the rest of us to become richer than sin."

She took a step closer, but made sure to keep herself well out of his reach. "I thought about what you proposed, but I still think I'd rather take a little smaller of a cut on a sure thing than get greedy and risk my life on the wrong side of a sucker's bet. So here's the plan. You've got one bullet in that pistol. Use it now against me or one of us . . . or use it on Mondoza's bodyguard. The man guarding Mondoza has been quick enough to keep that man alive this long, but I doubt he's much of a match against the Gunsmith."

Clint hefted the Colt in his hands. The familiar weight felt like the return of an old friend or a part of his own body. Just by the feel of it, he knew that it was too light to be fully loaded. There wasn't more than a single round in the cylinder, but the difference wasn't great enough to be sure there was one in there at all. Trusting Bonnie's word on that fact would have been the biggest sucker's bet he could have made at that point.

Feeling secure in her element and confident in the knowledge that she held the only winning hand at the table, Bonnie looked around at her men and then back at Clint. Her smile was subtle, but unmistakable. "Once you prove yourself to me in Arizona, you'll get a cut of the money. Not as much as the men that've been with me since the beginning, but you'll get a cut. As for all the profit we make along the way . . . well, I'm sure your conscience wouldn't allow you to partake in any of that."

Flicking his eyes over the crowd of outlaws that was slowly closing in around him, Clint waited until he sensed one of the men moving up behind him. He took a step back and felt the hard steel of a gun barrel jamming into the base of his spine.

"You really think Mondoza will appreciate it when he sees your bunch ride in and try to take over?" Clint asked. "You think he's lived this long by being an easy target?"

"His men are busy with the others in the tournament and are spread pretty damn thin right now. He's survived this long because of two things . . . nobody never knows exactly where he is at any given time and he hires the best gunfighters he can find to protect his ass."

That sly grin returned to her face, this time tainted with some of the bloodlust that had infected her men. "I know where to find him and I've got you to take care of those few men that might be good enough to stop us."

"You've got it all covered, don't you?" Clint asked. He settled against the gun barrel, which pushed it that much harder into his back. "Sounds like you've even got me figured out."

Now, Bonnie gave in to the smile and started laughing in Clint's face. "You don't really have much of a choice. If you slip up now, you know you'll die. In Arizona, those gunfighters will want to kill you just as bad as they want to kill us. You'll do what I need because that's the only way to survive. And," she added while looking at him with a glint in her eye that once again reminded Clint of the previous night, "I'm dead serious about cutting you in on Mondoza's money. He's worth twice the amount he's offering and once we roll in with his daughter as a hostage, he'll hand every cent over to us. You're not stupid, Adams. You'll come out of Arizona a winner just like the rest of us."

Clint studied her face for any sign that she was bluffing. Although he hadn't spent a whole lot of time with Bonnie Pearson, he felt as though he was talking to a completely different person than he had when meeting with her before. She'd been a cool, precise woman that reminded him of a soldier planning an attack. In fact, she'd made Andrea seem like the wild one in comparison.

But all of that changed.

When Clint looked at her now, he no longer saw Bonnie as someone he could work with or even convince to go his way. What he saw was a woman who'd probably wrested control of this gang from someone bigger and stronger than she was. The way she addressed her men and the promises she made told Clint exactly how she'd managed to keep control over so many killers. The fact that she'd managed to turn the tables on him and force him into this position was a good indication of how she kept that control always within her grasp.

In the time it took him to think all of this, two more of the gang's members had drifted in closer to him, all of them itching to be the first one to get a piece of his hide. Clint continued to pretend as though he was seriously considering her offer until he finally spotted the thing he'd been looking for out of the corner of his eye.

What he saw was a large Bowie knife hanging from the belt of the outlaw to his left. The blade hung in a leather sheath on the opposite side of that man's gun. Clint looked just long enough to confirm it was there before locking his gaze directly onto Bonnie's eyes.

In response to his stare, she simply shrugged and shook her head. "I watched you at the saloon the other night," she said. "You're good, but not good enough to get the drop on every one of these men."

Even from more than twenty feet away, Clint could see the angry twitch on Andrea's face when she heard mention of the saloon where her men had gotten killed. Clint looked over to her and carefully examined the way she was sitting, right down to the position of her hands and feet.

Bonnie held her ground, refusing to get any closer to him. "This is it, Adams," she said impatiently. "Are you gonna fire that gun now or in Arizona?"

Clint tightened his grip on the Colt and said, "I guess I might as well take it now since none of you are going to make it to Arizona."

THIRTY-NINE

The smug look on Bonnie's face dropped off the minute she heard Clint utter those words. Her eyes narrowed and for a split second, she looked as though she'd truly been caught off guard by his response. Rather than play her winning hand to its fullest, she'd looked into the face of a master gambler . . . and blinked.

With his back still pressed against the barrel of a gang member's gun, Clint spun his entire body around in a tight circle, using the pressure of the steel in his spine as a guide on where he could and could not go. By the time the outlaw got around to pulling his trigger, Clint had gotten mostly out of the way and felt only a burning scratch as a bullet tore through his shirt and skimmed along his skin.

Clint was still moving in one continuous flow, which brought him close enough to the man on his left for him to reach out and grab hold of the Bowie knife. The weapon actually felt small compared to Con's machete, but that made it even easier for him to lift it from its sheath and flip it in the air so he could shove his Colt into his belt and grab hold of the knife with his right hand while positioning himself in a sideways fighting stance.

Focusing in on one man at a time, Clint knew that the man who'd just fired his gun would be spending the next second or two adjusting his aim or pulling his hammer back for his next shot. Clint turned to face the outlaw whose knife he'd just stolen and watched as the man pivoted on the balls of his feet so he could move his gun into a better firing position.

By now, the first shooter was ready to pull his trigger again. Clint saw this and swiped his arm out and across, bringing the blade around into an arc of flashing steel.

When he turned to press the gun against Clint's side, the outlaw felt the deadly caress of the Bowie's edge slicing through his skin to open up his neck and spill a fountain of blood down the front of his shirt. The gang member staggered back a step, trying to say something as he went. All he could get out was a choking gurgle, which soon gave way to one last, rattling breath.

Even before the man to his right had time to fall down, Clint was pulling his hand back toward the one to his left. He could feel the warm flow of blood trickling down his arm as he brought the knife close against his side, twisted, crouched down low and stabbed straight out to bury the weapon into the second man's chest until the hilt slammed against ribs.

The man on the receiving end of the blade coughed up a mouthful of blood and let the pistol slip from his hands. At the same time the gun hit the ground, Clint yanked the blade free and cocked his arm back behind his head.

He knew he would only have one shot at this.

Even if he made it, Clint knew he'd still be in a whole world of trouble from what he'd figured to be eight remaining outlaws as well as Bonnie, herself. The gamble he was taking could very well be one of the sucker's bets that had been mentioned earlier, but it was all Clint could think of in the second and a half he'd been given to decide his fate.

With every bit of the strength he could push from his arm, Clint straightened his elbow and whipped the Bowie into the air. The blade spun in one . . . then a second tight circle as it covered the distance between his fingers and the intended target. It left a curved trail of blood as it passed that hung in the air like a smudge of crimson against a painter's canvas.

Within the last foot of the blade's journey, it sliced through the rope that had been binding Andrea's feet to her hands, and stuck into the ground between her legs. The handle wavered back and forth once it had found its mark and Andrea stared down at it as though she half expected the thing to hiss and take a bite at her.

At that moment, the world around Clint snapped back into full speed. The first thing he could hear over the pounding of his own heart was Bonnie's raised voice.

"Kill him!" she shouted.

Clint knew that he had less than a second to somehow dodge all the bullets that would be coming his way. Fortunately, everyone else in the camp had been just as confident as their leader that Clint would be too smart to make a move. Therefore, besides the two that had just been taken out with the knife, nobody else had cleared leather and were ready to shoot.

Of course, that little advantage had almost run out.

Running on pure instinct, Clint recalled hearing the heavy thud of the first killer's body dropping to the sand. He stepped back and to his left just in time to catch the body of the man who'd been stabbed before it tipped too far in the wrong direction.

With his left hand on the back of the dead man's collar, Clint held the body up so that it was positioned between himself and the incoming lead. Gunshots crackled through the open air and lead whipped past, every other round or so pounding into the dead outlaw, causing the corpse to jerk and twitch in Clint's grasp.

Clint dug the toe of his boot into the sand beneath the pistol the outlaw had dropped and when he quickly pulled his knee up, the gun popped into the air where Clint could grab hold of it by the handle. Once he was armed, he dropped down to the ground, letting go of the corpse, to be held up by the force of the bullets chewing into and chipping away at its flesh.

While snapping back the hammer of the gun, Clint

glanced over toward Andrea. She seemed to have gotten over the shock of Clint's first move and was taking advantage of the fact that her limbs were no longer so tightly constrained. After using her teeth to desperately pull the ropes around her wrists, she'd picked the knife out of the ground and used it to cut her remaining bonds.

Already, Clint could see the body starting to fall over and he braced for the impact it would make if it landed on his back. There were mounds of sand being kicked up around him as the incoming bullets drew closer and closer to his position.

Now was the moment where he would know if freeing Andrea had been the best or worst decision he could have made. Unfortunately, it was one of the only ones he could have made if he was going to get out of this desert alive. The distraction alone had given him some room to breathe. All that remained to be seen was whether or not he would be breathing after the next few minutes had passed.

The outlaw's body jerked to one side as another round punched through its flesh. The momentum spun him around to face away from the camp and the body began to drop down onto Clint, himself.

There were footsteps coming his way and Clint knew that if enough of them got a clean shot, his chances for survival would be about the same as those of the human shield he was about to be buried under. He tensed the muscles in his legs in preparation to break from cover, hoping that Andrea wouldn't be just another one of the people out to see him dead.

FORTY

When Andrea had seen the blade fly from Clint's hand and come straight toward her, she'd been too scared to move for fear of going the wrong way and putting herself in even greater danger. She knew in the moment it took for the knife to flash in the sun that she couldn't do much more besides sit and wait for the sharp fiery pain that was to fill her final moments.

Instead of feeling the sting of metal cleaving her flesh, however, she instead felt her arms and legs spring apart from each other as the ropes tying them together had been cut. She went about freeing herself while the rest of the gang focused on Clint and once the ropes were no longer a concern, she gripped the Bowie knife in hand and set her sights on Clint Adams.

Even with everything else that was going on, she was certain of one thing: Clint needed to be repaid for what he'd done.

At the same time, she would visit some payback to the rest of those that had either killed her men or turned them against her. But more importantly, it was time to get Bonnie Pearson out of her world once and for all.

The blood was rushing through her veins so fast that it sounded like a raging current in her ears. It made her head spin and her legs wobble when she went to stand up but once she was on her feet with the Bowie in her hand, every-thing seemed more in her control and the glimmer of hope made its presence known at the fringe of her consciousness.

Shots blazed through the air and the sound of lead pounding into flesh was loud enough to make even the most hardened of stomachs turn. Andrea looked quickly over to Clint just as he was lost beneath the pile of dead flesh that had once belonged to one of Bonnie's gunmen. She knew that Clint had seen her. She knew that he hadn't wasted the opening move of this fight just to try and kill her when she was already tied.

She also knew that if she was going to make it through this day to be alive for the next, it was going to be at his side.

Although the knife felt heavy and uncomfortable in her hand, Andrea grabbed it as tight as she could and charged toward the gang member that was closest to her. For the first few steps, the gunman was too busy shooting at Clint to notice what she was doing. Then, as her feet pounded against the tightly packed sand, Andrea watched him turn in her direction. Next, he swung the pistol around to blow her off her feet.

Andrea had heard stories from men fighting in the war about how their mind would become a blank when they were running toward certain death. She'd never been able to understand such a thing until she saw the cold, black eye of the gun barrel stare her down and her feet kept taking her closer toward it.

Just when she was certain the man was going to pull his trigger, she let out a primal scream and lashed out with the knife, swing her arm back and forth, up and down until she could no longer even lift the weapon.

Her eyes burned and her breaths felt like they were being ripped from her lungs by phantom hands. The shots were still going off around her, but when she took a moment to see where the rest of the gang was headed, Andrea realized one glorious fact.

She was still alive.

Looking down, she realized why she could no longer lift the knife. It wasn't from lack of strength, since she felt more potent now than she'd ever had before. It was because the blade was buried so far inside the outlaw's body that the hilt's guard had wedged in between two of the man's ribs.

Laying next to him was the pistol he'd been firing as well as a Henry rifle that she hadn't seen before. Andrea knelt down beside the body and picked up the pistol first. Not knowing how many shots were left in the cylinder, she held the gun out in front of her, aimed it at the biggest group of rival gang members and fanned the hammer just like Con had always told her *not* to do.

Although her accuracy was compromised, she was able to squeeze off the gun's three remaining rounds before any of the others even had a chance to turn around. When they did, one of the gunmen crumpled to the ground while the other was spun in a full circle, clutching a gaping wound in his side.

There was another set of gunshots coming from the other side of the camp, she realized. Her hopes were confirmed when she saw the outlaw next to the one she'd wounded pitch backward, a third eye staring blankly up at the sky. Through the space left where the man had been standing, Andrea could see Clint Adams peering at her over the smoking barrel of a pistol before throwing himself to the side to avoid the next round of fire.

Just before getting tied up like a prize calf, Andrea had been told all about what had happened the other night with Bonnie and Clint. She knew all about the men from her gang that Clint had shot and she also knew about what they'd done in the alley. She'd never been the mothering type, so if her men had gotten themselves killed, she didn't really feel any hard feelings about that. After all, even the way Bonnie told it, they'd been beaten in a fair fight.

As for what happened in the alley, that told her that Clint had been lying about what had happened to Con. She thought about that and quickly decided what she was going to do about it since there wasn't a whole lot of time to be indecisive. Grabbing hold of both of the guns she'd acquired, Andrea took a breath and charged into the fight.

FORTY-ONE

Once the body he'd been using as a shield was more holes than skin, Clint used all of his strength to toss the corpse into the biggest group of shooters that had gathered nearby. He couldn't tell how many more were left, but it did seem that Andrea had done her share of damage once she'd gotten herself free. Now all that was left to be seen was what she was going to do to him once she got a clear shot.

Clint was able to push the corpse hard enough so that it almost looked as though it was trying to take a few shuffling steps. Apparently, the sight of that alone was bad enough to cause at least three of the outlaws to stop firing long enough for them to scatter out of its way rather than be forced to touch the gruesome remains. Clint took full advantage of the opening and ran for one of the cooking fires, firing off a round along the way.

His bullet struck one of the men in the stomach, crumpling him over as the blood started to flow out of him in a crimson torrent. What had once been a barrage of gunshots had been thinned out somewhat within the last few seconds. Unfortunately, those that remained were taking more time to aim their shots instead of simply filling the air with flying lead.

Clint figured that he only had about two or three shots left in the pistol he'd taken. When he made it to the fire,

he kept right on moving until he was standing within five
feet of the newly freed Andrea Kinman. While he was making his way through the camp, he'd also been counting up
the outlaws that remained on their feet. Next to Bonnie,
there were two others along with the pair that were squirming wounded on the ground.

"Good plan, Adams," came a voice to Clint's left.

He didn't have to look to recognize the voice. "I was
hoping you'd like it, Andrea," he said. "Now how about
helping me finish it off?"

Demonstrating the same brand of composure under fire
that had kept Clint alive for so long, Andrea ran toward
him while firing to her side fast enough to cover herself.
The shirt she wore was torn in a few places and soaked
through with blood. There was also a chunk of her leg that
had been clipped away by a passing bullet.

"You're hit?" Clint asked once she got closer.

"It's not bad. Not enough to keep me down."

For the moment, the firing had stopped. Clint knew the
fire wouldn't provide any cover, but he had been hoping
the smoke might throw off the aim of some of the gang
members. The fact that no shots were being fired at all
made him more nervous than when his ears had been ringing from all the explosions.

"All right," Bonnie called out. "You've taken enough of
my men away to level out the odds. If we part ways here
we can all patch ourselves up and settle this once we reach
Rock Bottom."

Clint shook his head while checking over his gun. There
were two shots in the cylinder and at least five gang members still breathing. Looking over to Andrea, he could tell
she was also taking stock of her ammunition supply. When
she looked up, she held up three fingers. Apparently, those
were all in her pistol since she tossed the rifle to the ground.

Straightening up to his full height, Clint stuck the pistol
in his belt and walked around the fire so he could clearly
see who he was up against. "You still worried about that
damn tournament?" he asked in disbelief. "Why can't you

see that Mondoza is playing every one of you against each other?"

Holding his arms out to indicate all the bodies laying on the ground, Clint said, "He's already won. Your gang's practically gone and I'd wager that half of the rest of the killers on their way to Arizona have been taken down by the other half."

"I'm sure you're right," Bonnie said. "But that doesn't matter. I know where Mondoza is. All I have to do is get there and I can get that money away from him."

"How do you plan on that? You don't have your star hostage. You don't have your gang. And you don't have me to help get you through those bodyguards you were talking about."

Bonnie looked as though she might be angry enough to take a shot at him. The remaining men next to her waited for a sign to attack, but held off until they knew they were all going to fire at once. "I'll think of a way," she said. "I might not get all his money, but I'll get enough of it to set me up for the rest of my life."

Once again, Clint shook his head. "I can understand greed. I can even understand why you choose to live as hunted fugitives. I certainly don't agree with it, but I can't hold it against you because . . . you just don't know any better." That last sentence came out tinged more with pity than anything else. "You're animals," he added, looking around to Bonnie, the men next to her, and even the ones bleeding on the ground. "All of you."

Clint didn't know for sure what Andrea was thinking. At this point, he didn't want to waste time on guessing. What he did know was that, no matter how he tried to trick them or talk to them, no matter how he tried to steer them in the wrong direction, it wouldn't do any good. The carrot being dangled by Mondoza, whether it was real or not, was just too big for any criminal to pass up.

What struck Clint as funny was the fact that he'd been tempted by that same carrot. The only difference was that he knew when to let it go.

He didn't say any of this.

He didn't have to.

His thoughts were reflected in the tensing of his muscles and the squaring of his shoulders. They shone through in his eyes, which had become steely and focused. And just like the animals they were, every one of the outlaws could sense the oncoming storm that was brewing inside of him.

For a moment, the only sound in the desert was the dry wind blowing around them and the crackling of the flames. Bonnie started to say something, but choked back the words before they came out. She, too, knew the time for talking was over. The games were done. It was time to live or die.

Clint knew there was only one way to deal with dangerous animals. They needed to be put down.

The air was thick with smoke and the smell of blood. With each passing second, the tension became greater and greater. Andrea shifted on her feet, not used to staring straight at her opponents for so long without anything happening. The men laying wounded on the ground had stopped trying to push themselves into better positions and seemed content with playing possum.

As for Clint and Bonnie . . . they stared at each other until it seemed their eyes were giving off a tight stream of fire that shot from one and burned directly into the other. Clint could feel the impatience growing inside of her. In fact, he'd been counting on just such a response and was surprised that she'd held off this long without giving in to the violent impulses that obviously ruled her soul.

He was prepared to wait all day if necessary. In reality, he only needed to wait five more seconds before the first move was made.

Bonnie was the first one to go for her gun . . . just as she was the first one to take one of Clint's bullets directly in the chest.

From there, the desert once again erupted into a firestorm as outlaw fired on outlaw and lives came to a sudden, explosive end.

FORTY-TWO

As always, the desert reclaimed the campsite. Its silence rolled in like a fog to replace the clamor of gunshots and the painful screams. Its sands soaked up the blood that had been spilled and its heat pushed down on the shoulders of the only person left standing after all the shots had been fired.

Andrea Kinman stood with one hand clutched to her side, but refused to let the pain she was feeling force her off her feet. With exhaustion clouding her vision and her mind, she let the pistol drop from her hand since it was empty and useless to her now anyway.

She stared in disbelief at the incredible destruction that had been visited upon so many. It reminded her of pictures she'd seen of the war. Although it was on a smaller scale, it was no less horrible, even for someone who'd spent the better part of her life with a gun in her hand. Andrea turned toward the cooking fire and looked at the couple beside it, hoping that she hadn't chosen poorly when deciding which of those to help.

Clint knelt down over the figure of Bonnie Pearson. Besides taking the bullet in her chest, she'd also been shot in her shoulder and hip.

"You got your little war," Clint said to her. "Now you're going to do something for me."

177

Bonnie tried to laugh at him, but the effort caused her too much pain. Instead, she coughed up some blood and grunted with the pain that wracked her body. "I . . . I'm not feeling up to . . . doing much of anything."

Clint's hands moved gently over her body. He used a piece of his own shirt to clean away some of the blood and then tore off a few more strips to tie around her wounds to help control the bleeding. "We've got enough time to get you to the doctor." Looking closely at the wound in her chest, he started pressing a wad of material against it. "I wasn't aiming for your heart."

"Wh—what's that supposed to mean?"

"It means that I didn't hit it. But if we don't get moving soon, I might as well bury you right here."

The anger in Bonnie's face was long gone. In its place was fear tainted by not a small amount of pain. "What the hell can I possibly have to offer you?"

"Tito Mondoza. All I need to know is where he is. *Exactly* where he is."

"After all that talk . . . you're still going through with the tournament, huh? Looks like we're not so different . . . after all."

Clint finished up dressing her wounds and started scooping her up into his arms. "Just tell me along the way. I've still got to deal with those dogs you set loose on that town back there."

Andrea came to Clint's side and helped him set Bonnie onto the saddle of one of the nearby horses. "I'm still with you," she said. "I might as well see this through to the end."

"What about your father's tournament?" Clint asked.

She looked over at him and shrugged with a relieved expression on her face. "Why should I? You'll telling the law about where he is, won't you?"

Clint nodded.

"Then that's more than enough for me. I started this whole thing . . . this whole life I've made for myself . . . as a way to get back at him. Make him notice me. At least your way doesn't involve me getting shot at."

Clint led Bonnie's horse to where Eclipse was waiting.

After he climbed into the saddle, he started laughing. "If you didn't get shot at, maybe I should have been standing a little closer to you earlier."

Hopping up into her own saddle, Andrea smirked in her familiar way. "In case you haven't noticed, Bonnie hired some pretty lousy shots." Just then, as if stricken down by her own words, she twitched as a sharp jolt of pain lanced through her wound.

"I don't know about all of that," Clint said as the pain from his own wounds finally started to register on his system. "I'd say we got damn lucky."

"You should know better than to say something like that before the game is over, Mister Adams. I don't think we're going to have a very warm reception waiting for us in town."

Clint tied the reins to Bonnie's horse around Eclipse's saddle horn and gently touched his heels to the stallion's side. They made the trip without another word passing between them. Even Bonnie was too busy trying to stay upright to say much of anything. As they got closer to town, however, a wicked smirk drifted onto her face.

The sounds of random gunfire could be heard drifting down the street.

Certain that neither he or Andrea were up to another point blank shoot-out, Clint loaded up his rifle and tied Bonnie's horse off to a nearby post. He then looked over to Andrea, nodded and rode toward the crackling firefight.

When he arrived, Clint was fully prepared to be the newest target for most, if not all, of the outlaws. In fact, he was hoping to draw away as much fire as possible from any townspeople who'd been caught in the wrong place. Instead, what he found was something that brought him to a dead stop in the middle of the town's widest street. He couldn't keep his jaw from dropping open.

"What's the matter?" asked the man who Clint recognized as the one who'd been tending bar at the saloon. "You never see a posse before, señor?"

"Posse?" Clint asked incredulously. "I thought there wasn't even any law in this town."

"Maybe not officially, but we can take care of ourselves. I try to get the others to do this a long time ago, but these *banditos* come and go so quickly, we never have time to prepare. But now," he said while puffing his chest out proudly and slinging his rifle over his shoulder, "we have plenty of time. Especially when we hear the shooting out in the desert."

Clint took a good look around. Scattered about the street, some laying against buildings and others facedown in the sand, were all five of the men that Bonnie had sent in to sack the place. A few of the bodies were positioned as only the dead could lay, but at least three of them showed some faint signs of life. When he looked up from the scattered bodies, Clint saw the "others" that the bartender had been talking about.

They were looking out from all of the top levels of the nearby buildings and poking their faces out from some of the smaller ones as well. Each one of them stared out from behind firearms of every shape, size and condition. There wasn't a badge to be seen. Instead, these were locals defending their homes. All of them looked hesitant at first but once they saw the bartender talking to Clint in a friendly way, they lowered their guard somewhat.

"Where's Con?" Andrea asked.

When the locals saw her, they raised their guns and the sound of so many levers being worked rattled through the air.

Clint stepped in front of her and nodded toward the barkeep. "It's all right," he said. Turning to Andrea, he made sure to keep his voice down and his arms up high. "We can talk to the doctor about that when we drop off Bonnie. That's where I left him and that's where he's going to stay until some law comes through here to pick him up."

Although he'd been expecting some resistance from her, Clint was pleasantly surprised to see Andrea nod slowly and move her horse closer to Eclipse. "You'd better take my gun. These folks seem a bit high-strung right now."

Clint reached out to pluck the pistol from her holster and toss it to the ground. "You're not upset about Con?" he asked.

"No. He did a lot of good for me and the least I can do is make sure he gets out of this thing alive."

"He will," Clint said solemnly. "We've had more than enough executions here for one day."

The barkeep came up to Bonnie's horse and jabbed at the gang leader's knee with his rifle. "Should I take this one, señor?"

"That's all right," Clint replied. "We're all headed in the same direction anyway." Suddenly, his entire body felt as though it had been run over by a stagecoach. His lungs swelled painfully inside bruised ribs with every breath, and the several little nicks he'd taken seemed to be joining forces to create one colossal wound.

The bartender read this on Clint's face and ran for his saloon. "I'll get some water for you, señor. Phillipe," he called to a younger man standing behind him. "Go tell Doctor Lopez that he's got patients coming."

FORTY-THREE

Two weeks later, in a town just outside of Rock Bottom, Arizona, Andrea Kinman lay perfectly still in the bed of her rented hotel room and listened to the convoy of lawmen thunder past on their way to the home of Tito Mondoza. There had been plenty of activity nearby, as there seemed to be some kind of gathering at a ranch outside of town. But not until today had the law made a move all at once toward one specific hacienda.

Andrea could still feel pangs of dull pain going through her bandaged wounds. It didn't hurt as much as it had before they'd arrived in town. Even as the thundering of the posse's hooves got closer and closer with every minute that passed.

"I feel so much better," she said, while nestling her naked body a little deeper into the covers, which held on to her like a giant's hand.

The smile on her face grew even wider as something moved beneath the covers until it was directly on top of her. Working underneath the layers of cotton sheets and down blankets, Clint was careful not to touch any of the parts of her body that were still healing, but made sure to pay more attention to the tender areas that he'd gotten to know so very well over the last couple of days.

"Yes," he said softly, "you most certainly do."

Showing him the same amount of care, Andrea ran her hands over the back of Clint's shoulders and then through his thick tangle of hair. When she could feel his fingers tracing a gentle line down her stomach and all the way to the downy thatch of hair between her legs, she closed her eyes tightly and pressed her head back into her pillow while squirming ever so slightly beneath his weight.

When she spoke, her voice was almost too soft for Clint to hear. "It took the U.S. Marshal long enough to get off his ass and get over to that ranch we told him about. I just hope it really belongs to my father. Especially since I've never heard of it before."

"Oh, it's Mondoza's place, all right," Clint said as the tips of his fingers traced down along the plump pink lips between her legs. "I checked on it myself. He was there along with about half a dozen men who had prices on their heads that added up to a small fortune." Beneath the bedding, every breath Clint took was thick with the smell of Andrea's body. Her naked skin was all he could see and the soft contours of her flesh was all he could feel. "I was damn tempted to take one of them for myself and retire off the bounty."

"And why didn't you?"

"Because I had something better waiting for me back here," Clint answered as his lips pressed against her hot, moist vagina, which caused Andrea to arch her back and wrap one of her legs tightly around the back of his head.

Clint had been tasting her long enough for her to climax twice already. They'd been naked under those covers for the entire night and she was getting desperate to feel him enter her once more before the morning came. That was the deal, anyway. One more night together before she rode off to meet up with those deputies so she could spend some time with her father.

After all that had happened, Andrea knew she couldn't just walk away from it all free and clear. Clint didn't have to convince her. She was simply tired of running from the law, rival gangs and her father. She would face them all at once while facing up to what she'd done. But that wasn't until tomorrow. For now, there was still much better things to think about.

Clint ran his tongue over the slick, pink skin between Andrea's thighs once more before reaching up to pull the covers off of his head. With the blankets thrown back, he could see her body laying before him, a little battered after recent events, but still just as beautiful. Her round, firm breasts swayed as she adjusted her weight, the nipples hardening in the cool night air. A fine layer of goose bumps rose up along her stomach and down her legs as a smile slipped onto her face.

Even though he didn't agree with the way she'd lived her life, Clint couldn't help but admire the way Andrea had dealt with the way everything had turned out. After leaving behind what was left of her gang, she'd helped Clint tell the federal authorities enough about Tito Mondoza that would help them sweep up just about all of his higher-level associates. Even now, they were on their way to make arrests that would clean up this entire part of the country, and tomorrow they would even get to bring her in as well.

All because of the hell that she'd been through, thanks to her father's efforts to manipulate not only her but every other criminal in the southwest territories.

Clint's first reaction had been to deny Andrea's request for this last respite before paying her own visit to the law. But then again, if it hadn't been for her help with the Pearson gang, he might have very well been the one buried in that desert and Mondoza would have been celebrating a victory instead of watching as a brigade of lawmen came thundering down his throat.

But he had other, more selfish, reasons for granting her request. One of them was the way she rubbed her leg against his bare skin as she pushed her hips up close to his face. Another was the sweet taste of her juices as they dripped between her thighs and onto his waiting tongue. Another was the way she grabbed hold of him with a surprising amount of strength so she could roll him over and climb on top of him, straddling him and impaling herself upon his hard cock.

Andrea lowered herself down onto him, slowly taking him inside of her body until every inch of his penis was enveloped with her moist folds. Leaning forward and pressing her palms onto his chest, she clenched her eyes shut and rocked back and forth, moaning loudly as he began pumping up into her.

Clint sat up so that he could wrap both arms around her and feel the warm curves of her breasts pressed up against his skin. Their bodies moved together in a wriggling dance. Moving his hands down to cup her rounded backside, Clint lifted her up slightly and let her push back down again, her muscles straining to rub her hard little clit against his cock.

They made love with the passion that could only come from the knowledge that they would never see each other again. Their bodies pressed against one another, ignoring the dull pain of their wounds and striving to feel the rush of yet another climax, which made them both feel the life force pulsing gloriously through them.

Watching Andrea lean back and surrender herself to the pleasure he was giving to her, Clint was able to forget about all of the lines that had been drawn between them. Whether it be the line between lawful and lawless, killer and victim, hunter and prey, the borders between them melted away that night, leaving only man and woman loving each other until the next day when all the lines would be revealed again.

Watch for

DEAD AND BURIED

242nd novel in the exciting GUNSMITH series
from Jove

Coming in February!

J. R. ROBERTS
THE GUNSMITH